"I still have moments of rebellion," Lorrayne said. *"Like now."*

"Now?" Cole asked, the word shimmering between them. He thought of warm moonlit nights and soft, supple bodies. Kisses that went on forever.

Did her kisses do that? Had she ever felt that strong pull that drew a person into the eye of a hurricane? Or had she been like him, seduced by the promise only to be disappointed in the execution?

"What are you thinking?" Cole smiled.

"Nothing that has to do with the case."

"Yeah, me too." He took a breath. There was no mistaking the look in her eyes. Slowly he rose to his feet, slipping his hand to her cheek. "Want to get it out of the way?"

"You're on," she heard herself whispering.

The moment he kissed her, he *was* on. Completely turned on.

Dear Reader,

Once again, we invite you to experience the romantic excitement that is the hallmark of Silhouette Intimate Moments. And what better way to begin than with *Downright Dangerous,* the newest of THE PROTECTORS, the must-read miniseries by Beverly Barton? Bad-boy-turned-bodyguard Rafe Devlin is a hero guaranteed to win heroine Elsa Leone's heart—and yours.

We have more miniseries excitement for you with Marie Ferrarella's newest CAVANAUGH JUSTICE title, *Dangerous Games,* about a detective heroine joining forces with the hero to prove his younger brother's innocence, and *The Cradle Will Fall,* Maggie Price's newest LINE OF DUTY title, featuring ex-lovers brought back together to find a missing child. And that's not all, of course. Reader favorite Jenna Mills returns with *Crossfire,* about a case of personal protection that's very personal indeed. Nina Bruhns is back with a taste of *Sweet Suspicion.* This FBI agent hero doesn't want to fall for the one witness who can make or break his case, but his heart just isn't listening to his head. Finally, meet the *Undercover Virgin* who's the heroine of Becky Barker's newest novel. When a mission goes wrong and she's on the run with the hero, she may stay under cover, but as for the rest…!

Enjoy them all, and be sure to come back next month for six more of the best and most exciting romance novels around, right here in Silhouette Intimate Moments.

Yours,

Leslie J. Wainger
Executive Editor

Please address questions and book requests to:
Silhouette Reader Service
U.S.: 3010 Walden Ave., P.O. Box 1325, Buffalo, NY 14269
Canadian: P.O. Box 609, Fort Erie, Ont. L2A 5X3

Dangerous Games

MARIE FERRARELLA

Silhouette®

INTIMATE MOMENTS™

Published by Silhouette Books

America's Publisher of Contemporary Romance

SILHOUETTE BOOKS

ISBN 0-373-27344-4

DANGEROUS GAMES

Copyright © 2004 by Marie Rydzynski-Ferrarella

Books by Marie Ferrarèlla in Miniseries

MARIE FERRARELLA

writes books distinguished by humor and natural dialogue. This RITA® Award-winning author's goal is to make people laugh and feel good. She has written over one hundred books for Silhouette, some under the name Marie Nicole. Her romances are beloved by fans worldwide.

To
my readers,
with sincere thanks
for being there
Love,
Marie

Chapter 1

"Yes, yes, yes, I know," Lorrayne Cavanaugh declared loudly before anyone else had a chance to comment on the time as she burst into the kitchen. She was still dressing herself, her hair only half dry from the whirlwind shower she'd taken less than five minutes ago. To the eleven people already in the room, she knew she had to look like a tornado searching for somewhere to land. But they were used to that. They were her family. "I'm late."

"You're not late, honey," Andrew told her mildly, setting her plate down on the table. His gray-blue eyes met his youngest daughter's as she slid into her customary chair. "For lunch."

Not trusting the watch she'd just strapped on, Rayne glanced at the clock on the wall above the industrial stove.

"Dad, it's just a little past seven-fifteen," she pro-tested.

"More like seven-thirty," her oldest brother, Shaw, corrected. Amusement played on his lips. Rayne had been born six days past her due date and had been habitually late ever since.

Clay, her other brother, reached for a second help-ing of eggs and bacon. He spared her a fleeting glance. "Give it up, Rayne, we all know you're going to be late for your own funeral."

About to refill the decreasing supply of hotcakes, Andrew looked up sharply. As head of a clan that had, for the most part, all found their calling in some form of law enforcement, he took some things far more se-riously than the rest of them. He'd been to too many funerals in his time, seen too many good people cut down in their prime and put into the ground.

His eyes swept over the group he loved more than life itself. "There'll be no talk of funerals at the break-fast table."

"Right, much better topic at the dinner table," Rayne cracked. It earned her a chiding look from her older sister, Callie. Though she didn't move a muscle outwardly, inside, Rayne squirmed. "What, did I miss something?"

Teri, Clay's elder sister by a minute and a half, a fact she rarely allowed him to forget, laughed shortly. "The way you like to lounge around in bed, it's a wonder you don't miss everything."

There were two years between the sisters and if there was one thing Rayne hated, it was to be made to feel like the baby of the family. At twenty-five, she was hoping to have finally left that issue behind her. She was beginning to realize that the odds were she never would.

But that didn't mean she was about to accept it docilely. "That's a little like the pot calling the kettle black, isn't it?" They all knew that Teri loved to sleep in whenever she could.

With a sound of finality, Andrew placed the plate of hotcakes in the middle of the table, giving each of his daughters a warning look. Unlike Callie who'd never given him any grief and who'd now settled in with a good man, Teri and especially Rayne enjoyed burning the candle at both ends whenever the opportunity arose. There were nights when both or either of the girls would roll in only to have to leave for work a short while thereafter. He was utterly convinced that youth was wasted on the young.

"No bickering at the table—any table," he deliberately underscored before one or the other resorted to a sarcastic question.

"Nope, that's your domain," Rayne pronounced cheerfully just before she bit into the short stack she had liberally doused with maple syrup.

The battleground between father and daughter was familiar, if no longer so frequently tread. "I don't bicker, I impart wisdom," Andrew informed Rayne, then widened his scope. "The rest of you bicker with it."

"Not me, Dad." Rising, Teri crossed to her father

and kissed his cheek. "I know you just spout pearls of knowledge."

He looked at the plate Teri had left in her wake. She'd hardly touched any of it. He was a firm believer in breakfast being the most important meal of the day. "Is that all you're eating?"

It had never taken much to fill her. She was usually the first one up from the table. This morning was no exception. Besides, there were reports waiting for her, reports she'd put off filing. She had that in common with the rest of her siblings.

With a grin, Teri patted her flat stomach. "I eat any more and I won't be able to catch the bad guys."

"You could always try talking them to death," Clay suggested. It earned him a sharp poke in the ribs from his fiancée who sat beside him with the little boy he'd only recently discovered was his.

Ilene flashed an apologetic smile in Teri's direction. "He hasn't had enough coffee to seal his mouth yet."

Teri returned the smile. "Don't need to explain Clay to me. I had his number years ago, right, Clay?" She sent a penetrating, affectionate look his way before going toward the back counter where all of their weapons were carefully placed whenever they entered the house. With six of them police detectives, that made for quite an arsenal.

Rayne glanced in Teri's direction. The display of weapons was something they all took for granted, but sometimes she saw it through the eyes of an outsider, a role she'd once occupied within her own family.

"Enough hardware there to start a gun shop," she commented, shifting her attention back to her meal.

At any one given mealtime, there were anywhere from the three Cavanaughs who still lived in the house Andrew and Rose had bought on their fifth anniversary to the eighteen members and almost-members of the Cavanaugh family. Most of the time, the count was far higher than three. That was due in equal parts to Andrew's skills in the kitchen where the love of cooking he'd inherited from his own mother bloomed, and to the fact that they were a tightly knit family, a credit to the man who required their presence on a regular basis.

Rayne knew he was determined to keep them all together no matter what went on in their separate lives. "In family there is strength" was something he'd instilled in all of them.

The credo was fashioned after Rayne's mother's disappearance and in no small way helped to keep Andrew Cavanaugh going from one day to the next.

Sitting at her side, Callie leaned over and whispered, "It's the anniversary of Uncle Mike's death." The expression on her face told Rayne that Callie was certain she'd forgotten the date. Rayne said nothing because she had remembered. "He's a little touchy today. Try not to get under his skin too much, okay?"

Rayne bristled slightly. She would have done more so if it hadn't been for the fact that her oldest sister was right. In her time, she'd gotten under her father's skin far more than the rest of them combined. But then, she'd been the youngest when her mother disappeared, not quite ten at the time, and it had been an almost impossible adjustment for her.

She'd been the closest to Rose. It had taken her a while to get over her resentment toward the others who had had more time with the mother she adored. She'd felt cheated somehow, both by fate and her siblings who could recall more things, had more stories concerning their mother than she did.

It had taken her more time still to forgive her father for the argument that had caused her mother to leave the house that day in the first place. Heated words had been exchanged, and Rose Cavanaugh had gone for a long drive to cool off. It was a habit of hers. Except that this time, she'd never returned home.

A massive dragnet had been set in motion. Only three Cavanaughs had been on the police force then: Andrew, Mike and Brian. Her father and his brothers, aided by the entire force, had hunted extensively. Rose Cavanaugh's car was found at the bottom of the river the next day.

It took little imagination to piece the sequence of events together. Visibility had been poor that morning, with a low-lying fog enshrouding the winding road that was her favorite route to take. The car had swerved and gone over the side, plunging into the river just beyond. ''Death by drowning'' was the official verdict when the case was finally closed.

But Rose's body had never been recovered and so, Andrew maintained, she was still out there somewhere. Everyone outside of the family had given up hope of finding her alive years ago. And then, one by one, though none ever put it in so many words, everyone within the family had eventually accepted what seemed to be the inevitable conclusion: Rose Cavanaugh had perished that morning and her body had been swept out to sea.

Everyone within the family except for Andrew. Taking early retirement and leaving the force, he still retained the copious notes on the case, still periodically pored over them in hopes of seeing something that he hadn't seen the other thousand times he'd reviewed the file. Something fresh that would lead him in the right direction and to Rose.

He didn't seem like a man given to unfounded optimism, but he clung to his hope the way a drowning man clung to a piece of floating wood.

"I might be retired, Callie, but my hearing's not." Andrew turned from Teri as she took her leave and looked at his oldest daughter. "When you're a cop, or an ex-cop," he added significantly, even though he maintained that once a cop, always a cop, "death isn't something you like to joke about. It sits in that squad car or unmarked vehicle beside you every day, keeping you company whether you want it to or not." He looked at his late brother's children, Patrick and Patience. His door was always open to them as it was to his brother Brian's four. He couldn't love any of them any more than if they were his own. "Mike's death just reminds us of that." He felt himself tearing up and deliberately turned back to the stove, even though there was nothing left on there to cook. "I'll be going to the cemetery around three today. Any of you is welcome to join me.''

Rayne didn't wait for any of the others to say something. She knew they'd all be paying their respects, one way or another, when they could manage it during the day.

''I'll see if I can stop by, Dad,'' she told her father.

He looked at her over his shoulder and smiled. Everyone knew that there was a special place in his heart for the child who had caused him the most grief. ''That's three today, not tomorrow.''

''Yeah, yeah,'' she muttered, but without animosity in her voice. There had been a great deal of it once, but all of it had long since been leached from her. She'd come to terms with her demons. Gulping down her coffee, she snatched up a piece of toast to see her on her way. Her plate was immaculate.

Rising, she shoved the chair back into place. ''Well, if I'm going to claim some personal time today, I'd better put in a few hours first.''

Clay shook his head as he looked at his sister's plate. The last one at the table, she was technically the first one finished. This after two servings that had gone by at lightning speed. ''Damn, but you eat faster than any three people I know.''

Rayne gave him a knowing look before glancing sympathetically toward the woman next to him. ''That's because until Ilene had the clear misfortunate of hooking up and taming you, all you knew were exotic dancers who consumed a grape a day and pronounced themselves fat.''

The disgruntled look her brother shot her was reward enough for her. Rayne headed toward the collection of weapons on the counter. Hers had been there since last night.

"Cole Garrison's back in town," Patrick told his cousin just as she was about to strap on her holster.

It stopped Rayne in her tracks. Cole. She hadn't thought anything would bring him back to town. "What?"

Patrick looked at the others. It was clear that he had the inside track on this piece of news. "Yeah, I heard that he came back last night, driving a flaming red Porsche. I guess he doesn't hate money anymore."

Shaw gave a low whistle of appreciation. "A flaming red Porsche. Not bad for a black sheep."

Left in the dark, Ilene looked from Patrick to Shaw to Clay, waiting for enlightenment. Like the others, she'd grown up in this city, but she'd gone to a private school. "Cole Garrison?" The name didn't ring a bell.

"Someone I went to school with," Clay told her.

Shaw drained the last of his coffee. "The town's official bad boy."

"Except that it's his brother who's accused of murder, not him," Callie said as she pushed her plate back. "That makes Eric Garrison the new winner of the title, wouldn't you say?"

"Keyword 'accused,'" her fiancé, Brent Montgomery, reminded her.

As a criminal court justice, Brent had been the presiding judge who had placed bail for the younger Garrison. The amount had been high, but certainly nothing to cause Eric's affluent parents more than a momentary pause. It had surprised everyone when they hadn't come up with the money. Especially when they had gone through the trouble of securing Schaffer Holland, an excellent defense lawyer for him. Currently, Eric was still in lockup.

"There's an awful lot of evidence against him," Patrick pointed out.

Without realizing it, Rayne squared her shoulders. "Maybe."

Rayne saw the others all turn to look at her. She knew what they were thinking. That she was tilting at windmills again. Maybe that made her like her father, unwilling to accept something that everyone else took to be true.

Shaw put the obvious into words. "So you don't believe he killed Kathy Fallon?"

The blond crop of curls moved about her head like rays of sunbeams dancing along the wind as she shook it. "Not a hundred percent, no." It was a gut feeling, but she wasn't about to admit that to this crowd. She knew what they'd say. Gut feelings were instincts reserved for the older members of the family, not her. "Eric's spoiled and used to getting his own way, but he's not violent."

Shaw leaned back in his chair, his eyes pinned to her. "You went out with him, when? Seven, eight years ago? People change." And then he laughed as he gestured at her. "For God's sake, look at you. Eight years ago, your hair was blue, and so was your mouth.

We all became cops so we could cover your butt and keep you out of trouble.''

Rayne rolled her eyes. ''Thanks,'' she muttered sarcastically.

''Hey, every family's gotta have a goal that pulls them together,'' Callie told her.

She was backed up by a chorus of murmurings. Amusement played on Callie's lips as she looked at her watch. They all liked to tease Rayne, but there'd been a time when they'd been really seriously worried about the youngest Cavanaugh. A time when the future hadn't looked as good as it did.

''I think all of us better be heading out.'' Rising, Callie stopped to look at her almost stepdaughter, the child responsible for bringing her and Brent ultimately together in the first place. ''Time to get you to school, Rachel, and your dad to the courthouse.'' She looked at Brent. ''Justice can't make a move without him.''

A chorus of groans met her comment. ''Kiss him and get it over with already,'' Shaw ordered with a heavy sigh as he gained his feet and threw down his napkin.

''In front of all you Peeping Toms, no way.'' Taking charge of Rachel, Callie moved the little girl toward the door, then paused to nudge aside Rayne and pick up her own holster and weapon. ''You need a woman, Shaw.''

''I could fix you up,'' Brent offered, helping his daughter on with her jacket.

Shaw held up his hands to ward off the offer and any others that might be following in its wake. ''I'll find my own woman, thanks a bunch." He looked at the youngest Cavanaugh and attempted a diversion. "Besides, Rayne is the one you should be concentrating on. She's the wild one, not me."

"Not wild enough to want my own woman," Rayne deadpanned. Ready, she paused long enough to brush a kiss on her father's cheek. She figured if they both lived another fifty years, she might just be able to make amends for the way she'd treated him those awful years after her mother disappeared. "See you at the cemetery, Dad."

Andrew eyed her. Like all his children, Rayne had good intentions. But her follow-through left something to be desired. Still, she'd come a very long way from the tremendous handful she'd been. There were times during those years when he'd been convinced he'd be celebrating her twenty-fourth birthday standing over her grave rather than joining the rest of her family at a ceremony naming her Aurora's newest, youngest police detective. That had gone down as one of the proudest moments of his life.

He nodded, then winked. "I'm only half counting on that, you know."

Stepping out of the way as Clay retrieved his weapon, she fixed her father with a reproving look. "Where's your faith?"

"Plenty of faith," he declared, sinking the skillet into a sink of sudsy water. "That's why I'm half counting on it instead of not at all."

"Someday," Rayne told him as the rest of her family filed by on their way through the back door and to the cars that were parked outside, like as not blocking access to her own vehicle, "you're going to learn to count on me completely."

"I'm looking forward to that day, Rayne," he told her as she hurried out the door, the last as usual. "I surely am."

He glanced at the photograph on the seat beside him to make sure.

It was her.

Lorrayne Cavanaugh.

If his private detective hadn't taken the photograph and given it to him, Cole doubted that he would have recognized her. Certainly not at first glance. She'd changed a great deal since he'd last seen her. The clothes were no longer this side of outlandish, but tasteful and subdued. She wore a crisp light gray jacket over pants the same color and a light blue blouse that even at this distance brought out her eyes.

The most startling thing about Lorrayne's transformation was her hair. It was normal instead of the bright royal blue he recalled. She was a blonde now, like the rest of the females in her family. The last time he'd seen her, she'd worn it spiky. Now it was short, curly. Soft. It suited her.

So did the life she'd elected to follow instead of the hell-bent-for-leather one she'd led when he'd finally left town.

He supposed that gave them something in common. Once upon a time, while in their teens, they'd both been on a slippery slope, aimed toward inevitable self-destructive endings. But apparently she had reversed her course. Just as had he.

That gave them something else in common.

They had a third thing in common and it was that third thing that had brought him here to the Aurora police department's recently repaved parking lot, waiting for her to put in an appearance.

A private detective was all well and good, but he needed someone on the inside. Someone in the know. Before it was too late.

He sat watching her for half a second longer. Lorrayne emerged from her vehicle looking a little breathless, as if she'd pushed her car to the maximum to get here. Slamming the car door, she took long strides toward the front of the building.

The expression on her face dovetailed with the one clear memory he had of her. She'd come barreling into the high school cafeteria just after the last bell had rung and run smack into him. Her books had gone flying, but it wasn't that which had made an impression on him. And it wasn't her blue hair, either, although that had fleetingly registered.

It was her wide eyes as they'd look up at him that had imprinted themselves on his memory. That and the press of her body against his. Soft in the right places, firm in the rest.

But he'd been a senior at the time and she was just a freshman, utterly wild by reputation, even then. He'd wanted none of that, none of Aurora. What had driven him at the time was a desire for escape. All he had wanted then was to finish high school and to get the hell out of the town, away from his family. More specifically, away from his parents.

And now here he was, back again. Looking to right what he knew in his soul was a horrible wrong.

Funny how life turned out. He would have bet anything of the fortune he'd managed to accrue that he would never set foot back in Aurora again, no matter what.

But then, having his younger brother accused of murder had never been factored into that initial scenario.

"Lorrayne," he called as he got out of the cherry-red convertible. If she heard him, the woman gave no indication as she continued to hurry toward the front entrance. Cole lengthened his stride as he tried to catch up. She was small, but from what he could see, she was all leg. He raised his voice another decibel. "Lorrayne Cavanaugh."

Lorrayne.

No one ever called her Lorrayne anymore unless it was official business—or someone in the family trying to get under her skin.

With an impatient sigh, Rayne abruptly stopped and swung around to see who was calling after her. And narrowly avoided colliding into a man who smelled good enough to eat.

Chapter 2

It took Rayne less than a second to recognize him. The man she was looking up at was older now—ten years, if she recalled correctly—and perhaps even better looking now, if that were possible. But it was Cole Garrison, all right. She'd stake her next month's pay on it.

She would have known him even if conversation at the breakfast table hadn't found its way to the subject of his brother's arrest for suspicion of murder. There was just no mistaking those chiseled cheekbones, that artistically perfect cleft chin, those deep blue eyes or that mane of deep black hair that, though tamer and shorter now, still reminded her of the mane of a proud lion prowling over a domain he considered to be singularly his own.

The thing she didn't understand was what Cole was

doing here, calling out to her. She didn't even think he knew her name. Undoubtedly he was here to see his brother, but why was he trying to get her attention?

And how had he even known it was her? She'd only been thrown into his speech class that one semester when she was fifteen. That was ten years ago and she'd gone through a hell of a lot of changes since then. When she looked back at photographs from that period, she hardly resembled her younger self.

Well, whatever his reasons were, Rayne thought as she watched him cross through the parking lot, she was about to find out.

"You might not remember me—" His voice, deep, low, rumbled over her like a warming breeze in April.

"I remember you." A hint of a smile curved her lips. "Cole Garrison, right?"

Her eyes swept over the tan camel-hair coat he wore. It was a complete departure from the black windbreaker he used to favor. He was dressed like a businessman, not like the brooding heartthrob half the female population of Aurora High had mooned over. Time caught up to all of them, she supposed.

"Nice coat," she commented. Looking back, she realized that it was probably an inane thing to say, but she wasn't at her best when caught off guard in a social situation.

This wasn't a social situation, Rayne reminded herself. The man was clearly here about his brother. But again, what did that have to do with her?

"Thanks." Surprising her, he took hold of her arm,

giving every impression that he wanted to lead her off to the side. "Have you got a minute?"

She glanced down at his hand, her inference clear. She didn't like being led around, even by men who looked as if they could start up a dead woman's heart with one well-timed kiss.

Cole released her arm.

She remained standing where she was. "You want to see me." It wasn't quite a question as it was an astonished statement.

"Yes."

Her eyes never left his. "Not your brother."

He'd learned the value of planning things out. He wouldn't have been where he was if he hadn't. There were arrangements to be made. "I'll see him after I talk to you."

She shifted to the side, allowing several uniformed policemen to pass and enter the building. "Why?"

"Because I hear that you're not satisfied."

Rayne blinked, drawing a complete blank. "Excuse me?"

"You're not satisfied that Eric committed the murder. That he did what they arrested him for."

The pieces pulled themselves together. For a second there, when he'd said satisfied, her mind had leaped to an entirely different set of circumstances. Because she wasn't satisfied. Her life was good now, far better than it had been for many turbulent, troubled years, and her family was the best she could ever hope for, having stuck by her when even archangels would have bailed. But she was haunted by the feeling that there was something more out there.

She wasn't sure just what, only that it was something. And even though it had no shape, no name, not even a vague definition, that feeling called out to her.

Rayne was quick to rally together her thoughts. "I'm really not the one you should be talking to," she pointed out. "I'm not handling the case. I wasn't even the first officer on the scene."

That had been Richard Longwell, a patrolman she'd been through the academy with. They still maintained a friendship, although distant now since she had surpassed him by becoming the youngest detective on the force. It had driven an unspoken wedge between them.

The case belonged to Webber and Rollins, both of whom were very territorial when it came to their cases. "I can point out the detectives—" she began to offer, turning toward the entrance.

He cut her off. "No."

"No?" She was lost again. The man persisted in not making any sense.

This time, Cole moved so that his body blocked her immediate exit. He didn't want to talk to the first officer on the scene or the detective handling the case, at least not yet. Because facing them alone, he would be given the polite but disdainful treatment accorded to all family members. As far as the police saw him, he was the brother of a murderer. No matter what kind of a picture was painted for the public at large, once the police had a suspect, the burden of proof was on the accused's side. The accused had to prove he was innocent.

Cole needed someone involved, but not in the middle of it. He needed someone at least partially sympathetic to his cause. Which had brought him to a former hippie/wild child.

"No," he repeated firmly. "I want to talk to you."

They waltzed around in circles and as gorgeous as this dance partner was, she had a desk to get to and overdue reports to file. "At the risk of repeating myself, why?"

He gave her the same reason he'd just cited. "Because I heard that you don't believe Eric did it."

She'd done a little discreet nosing around on her own since Eric's arrest less than a week ago, but she certainly hadn't made her feelings public. As far as she knew, only her family was aware that she wasn't on board with what the D.A.'s office believed.

Unless the man was into mind reading, there was no way he could have known.

Her eyes narrowed as she looked at him. "And just where did you hear that?"

He waved a dismissive hand at her question. "That doesn't matter—"

"Oh, but I think it does." Her voice was deceptively calm. She didn't like not knowing things, especially when they concerned her. It irritated her beyond belief, chafing her like a stiff tag sewn into the back of a shirt.

His eyes darkened impatiently. "I don't have time to argue."

"Well then you've come to the wrong place," she informed him, "because my family tells me that I could argue the devil out of his pitchfork, if only in the interests of his own self-defense."

Cole did the unexpected. Rather than make a derogatory comment or utter an uncensored remark about what others referred to as her infuriating behavior, he smiled.

He smiled and she had the exact same reaction she'd had that very first time when she'd collided with him in the lunchroom. Butterflies. Big, fat butterflies with enormous wingspans that fluttered and tickled the edges of her entire inner structure with every movement.

For all intents and purposes, for a tiny instance in time, she was fifteen again. Fifteen and a veritable outcast, self-made or not, from every scenario life had to offer including the one that involved her own family. The only normal path she took was to have a crush, a crush that was born that day, only to die ignobly several weeks later when she'd overheard Cole making a comment about her to a friend of his. He said she looked like a clown. And she'd felt utterly and completely devastated, not to mention angry and humiliated. It took a long time for a phoenix to rise out of those ashes.

Funny what the mind chose to remember. She hadn't thought about that moment in maybe nine years or so.

"Did I say something funny?" she challenged, her

cool evaporating slightly as the memory of that day grew a little more vivid.

"Under any other circumstances, I'd pay to see a demonstration of that," he told her. "But right now—"

"Your brother's under arrest for murder and your parents won't put up the one million dollars to bail him out," she concluded. "Not exactly the Brady Bunch, are you?" God help her, but for one moment she felt smug. Her family would have never subjected her to the kind of public humiliation that Eric's had heaped on him. They would have sold the house before they'd allow her to languish in jail one extra minute.

He laughed shortly and this time there wasn't a hint of amusement. "More like the Addams Family without the humor."

The smugness vanished and she felt sorry. For Eric.

"Wow." The word escaped. She hadn't expected Cole to be this honest, especially not with someone who, high school alma mater aside, was a complete stranger to him. "So what exactly is it that you want from me—" she glanced at her watch "—other than making me late?"

"I'd like to talk to you when you get off duty."

"All right, fine, but I really can't help you," she warned. "It's not my case."

"So you said." His mind jumped ahead to a meeting place. Somewhere she'd feel at ease. He needed to win her over. "Do they still have that Mexican restaurant on 4th and Silver?"

"El Rancho Grande?" For a second she'd forgotten that he hadn't been around all these years. The restaurant had closed down after a fire had gutted it almost eight years ago. "It's gone. There's a Chinese restaurant in its place now. The China Inn."

Cole smiled again. He'd traveled over most of the lower forty-eight states. Whenever he came into a new city, one of the first things he'd do was find the best Chinese restaurant. It was a weakness he allowed himself.

"Even better. When do you get off?"

She was taking off early today, as she'd promised her father. Rayne didn't feel like sharing that with him. It was too personal. "How does six sound?"

"Earlier would be better," he told her honestly, "but six'll do."

She nodded then looked toward the electronic doors significantly. "It'll also be impossible if I don't get in there to start my shift."

He moved out of her way, then followed her up the stone steps. Rayne found herself struggling with an uneasy feeling that had no name, no reason for existence. It was the same kind of feeling she had when something was about to happen. But there was no stakeout here, no reason to want someone watching her back. She didn't get it.

Cole waited until she made it through the doors before walking in behind her. "Who do I talk to about seeing my brother?"

"That would be the desk sergeant." She pointed the man out to him.

"Thanks." As he began to walk toward the policeman, it was clear that he and the woman he'd stopped were bound in opposite directions. "By the way—" he tossed the words over his shoulder "—you look good. Electric-blue was never your color."

Her mouth dropped open. That was twice he'd caught her off guard.

She was definitely slipping, Rayne thought as she hurried down the corridor toward the elevator. But then, as she recalled, Cole Garrison had that kind of an effect on people.

Some things never change.

"Three-ten, not bad for you."

The lush green grass hushed her quick steps as she'd hurried across the field toward her father. His back was to her and he was kneeling over his brother's tombstone. She could have sworn he hadn't heard her approach.

The man still had ears like a bat, Rayne thought. But then, he'd always been one hell of a cop. It had taken her years to appreciate what she and the others had taken for granted.

"Not bad for anyone," she corrected as she reached him, "considering that the city's fathers in their infinite wisdom are rerouting Aurora's main thoroughfare, making it almost impossible to get across town. I'll have you know I left on time."

Andrew nodded. There was a chill in the air but he was bareheaded as he kneeled over his brother's grave. His hands were folded in front of him.

"I believe you." He looked down. There were two headstones there. Diane Cavanaugh was buried next to her husband. They were side by side, at peace in eternity the way they'd never really been in life. "It's not like Mike's got anywhere to go."

The depth of sorrow in her father's voice seemed immeasurable. At a loss as to what to do, Rayne placed her hand on his shoulder. "You okay?"

Reaching back, Andrew covered her hand with his own, remembering when that same hand had been so small, almost doll-like.

"Yeah, thanks for asking." Swallowing a groan, he rose from his knees, deliberately ignoring the hand she offered until he gained his feet. Only then did he glance at it. "You know, I can remember when you used to jerk that same hand away from mine. Wouldn't let me hold it, wouldn't let anyone steer you."

She pushed her hands into her pockets. The January wind was getting raw. She should have remembered her gloves. "Had to find my own way, Dad."

He nodded. There was no arguing with that, although he'd tried. "I'm glad you did, Rayne. And that when you finally found it, it was here, with us."

She knew what he wasn't saying, that he'd lived in fear that she would wind up in this lovely little cemetery, buried beside her relatives, years before her time. There was a period when she'd thought she would herself.

"Hey, why would I go anywhere else? Can't beat the food," she quipped.

Meals weren't what kept her home. She felt she

owed it to him. Owed him for years that were lost, years that she'd turned his hair gray and brought his heart to the brink of an attack. Truce was a good thing. It brought understanding with it.

And right now, she ached for what she knew he was feeling. It was hard to stand here and not feel the tears well up. Without realizing it, she laced her arm through his.

"Hard to believe it's been fifteen years already," Andrew murmured, still looking at the tombstone he and Brian had bought. Mike had left debts as a legacy to his family. The pension helped provide for Diane, Patrick and Patience, but pride had necessitated that they provide the burial for their fallen brother. "It feels like yesterday…" Andrew looked at his daughter. "Mike was a good man, Rayne. In his own way."

She wasn't sure if he was trying to convince her or himself. Of the three Cavanaugh brothers, Mike had been the one who'd made waves, who hadn't been satisfied with his life. Ever. Outshone by both his older and younger brothers, he'd let it eat at his self-esteem. He'd sought absolving comfort in the arms of other women and in the bottom of a bottle. Though Rayne was the youngest, she knew that there were times her uncle had taken his feelings of inadequacy out on his children and his wife. Which was why Patrick and Patience looked upon her father with far more affection than their own. He, along with Uncle Brian, had had more of a hand in raising them than Uncle Mike had.

She felt close to her father right now, vicariously

sharing a grief with him she didn't entirely feel on her own. "He was kind of like the black sheep, wasn't he?"

"Yeah." The word came out with a heavy sigh.

It was a term she'd silently applied to herself more than once. "You know," she said in a voice that was barely above a whisper, "there are times when I'm still afraid that I'm going to wind up just like him."

Andrew looked at her sharply. "Oh, no, not you, Rayne. He was the black sheep, or maybe just a gray one," he amended. "You were the rebel. Still are in your own way."

The look he gave her seemed to penetrate down to her very soul. It was all she could do to keep from flinching. She withdrew her arm, shoving her hands into her pockets again.

"Don't do that."

"Do what?"

"Look at me as if you had X-ray vision and could see clear through to my bones."

To lighten the moment, she pretended to shiver. But the effect of her father's steady gaze was no less real. The way he could look at any of them would easily elicit a confession to some slight wrongdoing when they were growing up. She used to imagine that her father could force confessions from hardened felons just by giving them *that* look.

"It's not your bones that tell me what you're like, Rayne," Andrew told her gently, "it's more of a case of memory."

"Memory?" She felt a familiar story coming on.

As much as she'd bristled over hearing stories when she was younger, she'd come to welcome them now. They were a comfort to her and a way of bonding with her father.

"Your mother was just like you," he recalled fondly. "Always bent on doing her own thing. Always had to find her own way to the right conclusion."

This was nothing she hadn't heard before. As was the note of bittersweet sorrow in her father's voice. For a second she was tempted to put her arms around him and hug tightly. But there was still a small portion of her that resisted.

"You miss her a lot, don't you?"

He sighed and nodded. "More than words can say, Rayne. More than words can say. I miss them both a lot." He looked down at the tombstone. "The difference being is that I know Mike's gone."

She shut her eyes, knowing what was coming. It was a path she walked herself more times than she cared to think, but to hold on to irrational hope wasn't healthy. He was the only parent she had left and as much as she declared herself to be full grown and independent, she didn't want to lose him.

"Dad—"

He laughed softly to himself. "You're going to tell me not to start again. But I'm not. I'm just maintaining the same steady course I always have over all these years." He looked at her, debating. Then he made his decision. She needed something to make her a believer again. And maybe he needed someone else to believe besides himself. "I haven't told the others, but I found your mother's wallet."

She stared at him, dumbfounded. "What? When?"

He fell into police mode, giving her the highlights. "A little more than a month ago. Just before Thanksgiving. Homeless man had it in his shopping cart. He was dead, so he couldn't be questioned. I don't know where he found it and the lab couldn't get any readable prints off it, but it was your mother's." He saw the doubt returning to Rayne's eyes. "It had her license and pictures of all of you in it. She had that in her purse on the day she left the house.

"I went to see that homeless man in the morgue. He didn't look like any deep-sea diver to me, which meant that he found the wallet on dry land."

"Which means what?" Rayne asked. "That she was mugged? That her purse washed up on shore?" She took hold of her father's shoulders, desperately wanting to get through to him. This was killing both of them by inches. "Dad, just because you found her wallet doesn't mean that you're going to find her, or that she's even—"

He cut her off sharply. "It means exactly that, Rayne. She is alive and we're going to find her. It's as simple as that."

He made her want to scream. "Dad, you have to move on with your life."

"I *have* moved on." He struggled not to raise his voice. He'd moved on from one day to the next, accumulating fifteen years. Getting things done. "I'm not sitting in any closet, or staring out the window for days on end. I've raised five kids, had a hand in raising a couple more and even now make sure that everyone's fed, warm and thriving to the best of my ability.''

He looked down into her eyes, fighting to keep his voice from cracking. ''But don't ask me to stop believing that someday I'm going to see her, see your mother walking toward me. Because the day I stop believing in that is the day I stop breathing. She was my life, Rayne, my every breath. My mistake was in not letting her know that.''

A smile played along her lips. ''You don't make mistakes, remember?'' And then, breaking down, Rayne embraced him. ''God, Dad, I hope that someday someone loves me just half as much as you love Mom.''

For a moment he held her to him, just as he had when she was small. A lot of time had gone between then and now. ''They will, Rayne, they will. Or I'll personally fillet them.''

He was rewarded with her laugh. Andrew stepped back, glancing over his shoulder. He saw three men walking in their direction.

''Okay, dry those tears, here come your brothers and Patrick.''

Straightening, she wiped away the telltale signs of rebellious tears before turning around to face the approaching threesome.

She tossed her head, her hair bobbing about her face like golden springs. ''You're late,'' she declared with no small amount of glee.

It earned her a shove from Clay.

"There'll be no fighting at the grave site," Andrew informed them.

"Yes, Dad," Clay and Rayne dutifully chorused before they grinned at one another.

Chapter 3

It was a room that reeked of desperation and despair. Furnished only with two chairs squared off on either side of a scarred metal rectangular table, its gray walls—the hue of an old buffalo nickel—provided the only color within the small area. There were no windows, only a single door. A door with a guard standing on the other side.

Cole watched as his younger brother was brought in. Clad in a faded orange jumpsuit, Eric rubbed his wrists the moment the required handcuffs were removed.

He looked bad, Cole thought. A mere shadow of the laughing, carefree boy he'd once known.

Anger welled within his chest. Anger at his parents who should have stopped this years before it happened. Anger at Eric for choosing the path of least resistance, for squandering his life and allowing himself to be devaluated this way.

Cole had pulled strings to see his brother inside this room. Ordinarily the room was used only by lawyers for consultations with their jailed clients. Anyone else was required to meet with prisoners in a communal area with a soundproof length of glass separating them and words echoing through a phone line.

He knew Eric. Eric had trouble dealing with restrictions. The very thought of bars around him fed his claustrophobia.

It surprised him to see how old Eric looked. He'd left a boy behind. The person standing uncertainly before him was a hollowed out man.

They'd always been worlds apart, he and Eric. He'd been born old. Eric, he'd thought, was destined to be eternally young. His brother was more childish than childlike, but it had had its appeal, especially among the kinds of women Eric gravitated toward.

For Kathy Fallon, the appeal had apparently worn thin. Cole knew without being told that Kathy's leaving had been difficult for Eric to accept. His brother was accustomed to people liking him, seeking him out for a good time. Eric always had an endless supply of money and loved parties.

There was no party for Eric here.

There might not be one for a very long time if all the wheels he was trying to put into motion ground to a halt, Cole thought.

The expression on Eric's face was equal parts surprise and relief when he looked at him.

Cole pulled his own chair out and nodded toward the other chair, indicating that Eric do the same. The metal legs scraped along the floor. Eric fell limply into his chair. His eyes looked eager as they fastened themselves to Cole's face.

"You came."

"You're my brother," Cole replied simply, hiding the fact that a wealth of emotions, too many to count, were tangling up inside of him.

It had been that way ever since Eric's lawyer had called to tell him that Eric had been arrested and was asking for him. He'd booked the next flight out of New York and spent most of the time on the phone, planning, gathering what information he could. By the time he'd landed late last night, Cole had had as much of a handle on things as he could.

Long ago, he'd learned to rely first and foremost on himself.

Eric's knuckles were almost white as he clenched his hands into impotent fists in front of him on the cold table. "I didn't do it. I swear I didn't do it."

His brother's voice was almost quivering as he begged to be believed. Cole shook his head. "I'm not the one you have to convince."

Eric's eyes widened. The brown orbs were badly bloodshot, a testimony to the recreational drugs that had found their way into his system. He was in withdrawal and it was taking a toll on him.

"Then you believe me?"

Cole knew his brother was many things, many of them unflattering, to say the least. But a murderer wasn't numbered among them. He'd known that even as he'd listened to the lawyer's recitation of the police report. "Why do you look so surprised?"

"Because everyone thinks I did it." Eric's voice nearly cracked with hopelessness. "Mother and Dad think I'm guilty."

Cole hadn't been by to see his parents yet. He was putting off a visit until it became absolutely necessary, or until he had the stomach for it. Other than giving their seed, neither Lyle nor Denise Garrison had ever been parents in any real sense of the word.

He didn't have to see them to know how they felt about all this. If there was any doubt in his mind, the fact that neither had put up bail for Eric was proof enough.

"They only think you're guilty of bringing shame to the almighty Garrison name." An ironic smile twisted his mouth. "Something great-great-granddad beat you to in his youth, but they don't want to acknowledge that." The fact that the family money had been accrued by a robber baron was never spoken of. Cole took a deep breath, bracing himself. "So, what happened?"

Shoulders that were far less broad than Cole's rose and fell haplessly beneath the orange jumpsuit. "The police arrested me."

"Before then."

The expression on Eric's face was tortured as he tried to remember. "I was at a party. I think." Frustration ate away at the thin veneer of his confidence. "I don't know, I passed out."

"At the party?"

Eric looked as if he was taxing his brain. "No, alone I think. There was this girl—but she wasn't there when I came to," he concluded helplessly.

"Where did you come to?" Cole enunciated each word slowly. In a way, he thought, he was dealing with a child, a child that was too frightened to think. Whenever Eric became afraid, he made less and less sense. He remembered that from their childhood.

Eric screwed his face up as he tried to think. "At my place."

So far, Eric's story didn't sound promising. The lawyer, an old family friend with tepid water in his veins, had warned him off the record that the facts looked pretty damning.

"Did you see Kathy anytime that evening?" When Eric didn't answer, Cole leaned forward across the table. "Did you?"

Like a child caught doing something he knew he shouldn't, Eric hung his head and stared down at his hands. "Before I went to the party." Then his head jerked up. "But she was alive when I left her. She was screaming at me."

"That's because you weren't supposed to come around anymore," Cole reminded him. "She'd gotten a restraining order against you." It had happened less than two months ago, after Kathy had broken it off with his brother. Quinn, the detective he'd hired, had told him that Eric hadn't been able to reconcile himself with the fact that they weren't together anymore.

"I didn't think she meant it." An urgency rose in

his voice as he tried to make Cole understand. "This is the first woman I ever really cared about. I loved her, Cole. And then just like that, she said it was over." Color flooded his cheeks. "It couldn't have been over. I didn't want it to be over. Why did she have to call in the police?"

"You were stalking her, Eric." Quinn had been very thorough in his summary, faxing him the details rather than wasting time with a phone call.

"I wasn't stalking her, I was trying to win her back. I don't have any practice with that," Eric lamented. "I never wanted anyone back before." He hit his chest with his outstretched hand, the reality of it all not making any sense to him. "This was me, Cole, everybody likes me."

Eric honestly believed that, Cole thought. In some ways, his brother was still very much an innocent, not realizing that what most people gravitated toward was Eric's money, not his company.

"Not everybody, Eric," he said quietly.

A storm cloud filtered over his face. "You mean, Mother and Dad?"

Cole truly doubted either of his parents liked anyone, not even themselves. But that wasn't the issue here. "No, I was thinking about the person who's trying to frame you."

The simple statement hit Eric with the force of an exploding bomb. "You think that's it? Somebody's trying to frame me?"

Eric's fingerprints had been found all over Kathy's apartment. More damning was the ring that had been found in Eric's apartment. The ring with Kathy's blood on it. An impression of it had been left on her face where he'd hit her. Something else Quinn told him that Eric didn't recall. His brother's memory of the night in question was filled with more holes than a package of Swiss cheese and he'd claimed to have given Kathy the ring because she'd admired it weeks ago.

"Well, it's either that, or you did it." He saw Eric drag his hand erratically through his hair. Nerves? Fear? Was he wrong? *Had* his brother killed the woman in a fit of jealousy? He felt clear down to his bones that Eric wasn't capable of something like that, but maybe he was letting the past color his vision. "Eric, is there something you want to tell me?"

Eric covered his face with his hands. "I don't remember." When he looked up, panic lit his eyes. "Cole, I don't remember. I get these…" He licked his lips, as if they were too dry to produce the words he was looking for. "Blackouts the doctor calls them…"

Cole never took his eyes off his brother's face, trying to read every movement, every nuance. Looking for answers to questions that hadn't been formed yet. "You've been to the doctor about this?"

Eric's head bobbed up and down. "Last May. Dad insisted."

Cole frowned. So there was someone to testify in a court of law that Eric had periods where he blacked out, where he didn't remember what he did. Cole felt as if he was staring down into an abyss.

"Cole, is it bad?"

Cole folded his hands in front of him. "I won't lie to you, Eric, it's not good."

Eric bit down on his lower lip to keep from whimpering. A tiny bit of noise escaped anyway. "Then I'm screwed?"

"No," Cole said firmly, "you're not." If his brother was innocent, he was going to prove it. Even if he had to resort to the proverbial movement of heaven and earth to do it.

Eric grasped his hand between both of his. Eric's hands were clammy. "You're going to get me out?"

Cole gave one of Eric's hands a squeeze, trying to infuse a little courage into his brother. "I sure as hell am going to try."

Eric's eyes shone with a sudden onset of tears. "You're the only one, you know, the only one who cares what happens to me. You always were."

Any minute, Eric was going to go to pieces. He knew all the signs. Like the time there'd been a locker search and the principal had found a nickel bag of marijuana in Eric's locker. The only way to save his brother was to say that he'd been the one to leave it in Eric's locker. But this was a great deal more serious than a three-week suspension.

"Don't fall apart on me, Eric. I need you to focus, to keep it together. Try to remember what happened that night, what you did and, more important, who saw you do it. Work with Holland, he might be a friend of Mother's and Dad's, but he's also one of the best lawyers around." Cole saw that none of this was getting through to Eric. He looked like a frightened rabbit.

"I'm going to see what I can come up with on my end."

Eric brightened. "You're my only hope, Cole."

Truer words were never spoken, Cole thought, leaving the rest unformed even in his mind. "We'll get through this, Eric. We always have before."

As Cole rose, his brother suddenly leaped to his feet. Coming around the table, Eric threw his arms around him and embraced him.

Cole had never been a demonstrative man by nature. He'd been through too much, seen too much at home to leave the door to his emotions unlocked. It was the only way he had managed to survive. But this was his brother and he loved Eric beyond any rhyme or reason.

After a beat Cole closed his arms around his younger brother and gave him what he knew Eric needed most at this moment. He needed to have someone love him.

For a long moment Cole did nothing, said nothing, only hugged him.

"I'm scared, Cole," Eric sobbed against his shoulder.

He knew that. Knew, too, that he was scared for him. But that was something he wasn't about to admit out loud. Eric needed to think that his older brother was a rock. Confident. Unafraid.

So he perpetuated the illusion. As he always did. "Hey, it'll make for a good story once it's behind you. And it's going to be behind you," he promised with conviction. Eric pulled his head back and Cole saw a hint of a shaky smile forming. "It'll give you something to impress people with."

Ever since Eric'd been in elementary school, his brother had been a weaver of stories, colorful stories that drew the listener in and bonded him with the teller. It was his one gift.

Eric nodded, fighting more sobs. "Yeah," he mumbled, trying to muster up feeling, "a good story."

Crossing to the door, Cole knocked once. The next moment, it was being opened and the same guard that had accompanied Eric into the room stepped inside. He was holding handcuffs.

"I'll be back soon," Cole promised. He fought a sinking feeling as he saw Eric being handcuffed again. Unable to watch, Cole walked quickly out of the room.

Rayne pulled up the hand brake on her secondhand Honda. It'd been a gift from her father when she'd graduated from the police academy, coming to her with more than forty thousand miles on it. She intended to keep it until it was pronounced dead by Joe, the mechanic they all used.

The lot behind the restaurant was crowded and it had taken her two passes before she'd found a spot to park. Getting out and locking the door, she wasn't completely sure what she was doing here.

She supposed, as she made her way to the large red entrance doors, that it was curiosity that brought her. That, and the fact that she felt as if she were taking a dare. She wasn't the kind to back away from a challenge. Ever. And there'd been a challenge in Cole Garrison's deep blue eyes.

The cold and noise of the outside world faded the instant she crossed the threshold. A soft, subdued murmur of voices greeted her as did a petite Asian hostess dressed in what Rayne took to be authentic Chinese garb. The menu the woman held in her hand was almost half as large as she was.

"Table for one?"

"No, I'm supposed to be meeting someone."

Rayne looked past the woman's shoulder and scanned the subtly lit room. She spotted Cole sitting in a corner booth located just beyond an incredibly large fish tank. An array of lights broke through the water, shining on a variety of saltwater fish.

But her mind wasn't on fish, it was on the man she'd come to meet. Setting down his menu, he sensed her entrance and looked in her direction.

Even at this distance, his eyes seemed to lock with hers.

"Him," Rayne told the woman, pointing Cole out.

The woman inclined her head, turned on a very high, very thin, heel and led the way to the rear of the dining area.

Cole half rose as she approached the table and remained that way until she'd taken her seat. Old-fashioned manners. Who would have thought?

"Sorry I'm late," Rayne murmured, accepting the menu from the hostess without looking.

He wore the same clothes he'd had on earlier, except for the coat, and looked as crisp and relaxed as if he'd stepped out of some magazine meant for the discerning man. Obviously his day had gone better than hers. In between her trip to the cemetery, she'd wrestled with a mountain of paperwork, then got called away to investigate a shooting at a convenience store. If she had her way, all convenience stores would be outlawed. Or at the very least, renamed inconvenience stores.

She was more than half an hour late. It was obvious by the set of his jaw that he didn't like waiting. His tone did little to mask his shortened temper. "I was beginning to think you'd changed your mind."

"I don't leave people dangling," she informed him crisply. "When I say I'm going to do something, I do it. Just not always in the allotted time frame," she added after a beat.

She didn't like being late, she really didn't. Whenever possible, she went out of her way to try to be early. But most of the time it was as if the forces of nature conspired against her, by either causing her to sleep through what was the loudest alarm she could find, or by conjuring up extra vehicles on the freeway, or by arranging things so that they went awry.

"Admirable quality." He saw his waiter approaching their table. "Do you want to order?"

Rayne nodded. She knew exactly what she was in the mood for and gave her choice to the waiter, passing on the drink. Cole, she assumed, had already ordered. "Been waiting long?"

"I was here at six."

Which meant that he'd been sitting here for half an

hour. She refused to feel guilty about that. She wasn't the one repaving the main thoroughfare. "Maybe you should have picked an Italian restaurant. At least you could have nibbled on the bread sticks."

"I would have ruined my appetite. Chinese food is worth waiting for." He paused only long enough to allow his eyes to slide over her. "As were you."

"Someone else might call that a line."

"Someone else doesn't know me." He waited until the waiter, who'd returned almost instantly with their orders, set the plates down and withdrew. "I don't waste my time with lines."

Once the meal was in front of her, she realized just how hungry she was. The only thing supplementing the huge breakfast she'd had was an energy bar she'd found in the back of her desk. It had been far too long since her last meal. No wonder she felt a little light-headed.

"Then you're nothing like Eric," she told him as she dug in.

"Not really," Cole said, noting Lorrayne was a woman who ate instead of picked at her meal. Considering how small she was, he had to admit he was pleasantly surprised. "How well do you know my brother?"

The information was at the tips of her fingers. The D.A. had already asked her the same question. She wasn't the only Cavanaugh who was acquainted with the accused. Because her cousin Janelle, an assistant in the D.A.'s office, had also gone to school with Eric, the D.A. hadn't assigned her to the case.

"We dated a couple of times in high school." Then, in case Cole was attempting to recall whether he'd been aware of that sequence of events, she told him, "You'd left town by then." He looked surprised that she would have known something like that. "You took up a great deal of the conversation on our first date. Eric idolized you. Said he wanted to be just like you, but didn't have the discipline."

And then she smiled.

He found the look disarming and infinitely appealing. He wondered if she used it as a weapon. "What?"

"As I recall, you didn't have all that much discipline." She'd made short work of her egg roll and was onto to the main course without missing a beat. "Didn't you almost get expelled once?"

"Minor misunderstanding. They found some marijuana in Eric's locker that was mine."

"Was it?" Her tone was mild. A little too mild in his opinion.

"That's what I told the principal."

Her eyes met his. "That's not what I'm asking."

He'd never bothered telling anyone the real story. There didn't seem to be a point. "Eric wouldn't have been able to put up with suspension. He probably would have dropped out." Not that graduating high school and going on to college had managed to do very much for his brother. It had been just another excuse to continue floating. Cole had hoped otherwise.

"So you took the fall for him. No wonder he thought of you as a saint." She stopped to take a sip of her tea. "You didn't drop out," she recalled.

He smiled more to himself than at her. "Someone convinced me I needed an education."

"Oh?" Interest peaked, she cocked her head. "Someone in the Addams Family?"

He grinned. The woman had remembered the analogy he'd made earlier. But there was no way that his grandfather could have been considered part of the circus that comprised his family except in the strictest sense of the word "family."

"My father's father. He was a black sheep, like me." A fondness came into his voice. It was the money his grandfather had left him that now allowed him to do what he felt was his calling. And to be his own person, unlike Eric who had always been tied to his parents' purse strings. "He was the one who told me that the way a black sheep keeps from getting sheered is by learning to stay ten steps ahead of everyone else."

"And do you?" she wanted to know. "Stay ten steps ahead?"

He knew she was pulling information out of him. More information than he was accustomed to volunteering, but for now, it amused him to watch her at work. So he played along.

"At least five."

Because she identified with what he was saying, she laughed softly. It wasn't all that long ago that she'd followed the same path. "That sounds more like the credo of a con artist than an educated man."

He thought of the paths he'd followed before he'd settled down to his present way of life. He'd been a little of everything, including a mercenary for a while, taking on all life had to give just to feel something, anything. Adrenaline coursing through his veins when his life was on the line in the jungles of Bogota was as close as he got to experiencing anything.

"I'm guilty of both."

She was surprised he admitted it. "And are you still a con man?"

His smile locked her out. "At present, I'm a respected businessman."

But she apparently wasn't one to accept a locked door and back away. "What sort of business?"

He put it in the most nebulous of terms. "I buy houses that need work—then work."

She'd done a little homework before coming to meet him. It helped to have an in with someone in the IRS. His last form had referred to him as a builder. And there had been numerous charitable contributions cited, as well. "You make it sound simple."

He shrugged as he finished his main course. "At bottom, most things are."

Finished, as well, she pushed aside her plate and reached for her fortune cookie. "Interesting philosophy. But it's usually hard to get to the bottom."

He watched her long, slim fingers crack the golden shell. "Never said it was easy." He indicated the paper she cast aside. "Aren't you going to read your fortune?"

"I don't believe in the clairvoyant powers of a cookie." But because he was watching her, she glanced at the slim paper. *You will find love soon,* it read. *Yeah, right.* She raised her eyes back to his face. "What do you want with me?"

The prepared answer was not the one that rose in his mind. The word "want" all but shimmered in front of him. A man could want a woman like Lorrayne. She was more than pleasant to look at, the rebelliousness in her eyes having not quite been tamed by the position she'd assumed. Everything appealing and attractive had conspired to join forces within Lorrayne Cavanaugh. The last job in the world he would have said she'd been drawn to was that of police detective.

But a police detective was exactly what he needed right now. If there were other needs unexpectedly raising their heads, he would just have to ignore them.

He was fighting the clock. The D.A.'s office was out for blood. Eric's blood. Even if his brother wasn't guilty, everyone thought he was and appearance was enough to appease the masses.

He had to change that. But he couldn't do it alone.

"I want you to help me prove that my brother's innocent."

"In case you haven't noticed, I'm part of the Aurora police force."

She began to refill her cup, but he took the teapot from her and did the honors himself. "I noticed. That's why I came to you."

Ignoring the tea, she began to slide out of the booth. "I'm afraid there's more than a slight conflict of interest here."

Cole took hold of her wrist. "Just hear me out."

Training told her to shake off his hand and to keep

walking. Instinct told her to stay. She'd learned that the Cavanaugh instinct was more than just a pleasant myth her father liked to regale them with. It was based on the truth. They could all testify to that.

With a sigh, Rayne settled back in the booth. "Okay, talk."

Chapter 4

Cole opened with his best offense. "You think my brother's innocent."

She realized that she was still letting him hold on to her wrist. Rayne pulled it away, dropping her hand in her lap. "What I think or don't think doesn't matter and it certainly doesn't concern you."

He frowned. "Don't pull that 'them versus me' garbage on me. It didn't do you any good then and it's not going to work now."

The man looked as if he was disappointed with her, but Rayne hadn't a clue what he was talking about and she didn't particularly care for his tone. "Then?"

He didn't think that he needed to explain this part of it to her. She knew what she was like back then better than he did. "In high school. When you paraded around as if every day was Halloween because you were trying to get everyone as irritated and angry at you as you were with them.''

Her eyes narrowed. ''So you got your degree in psychiatry, is it? Or was this part of your con man education?''

He wasn't about to allow himself to be baited. There was too much at stake right now. He didn't appreciate her making him feel as if he was standing on the other side of the fortress, trying to get in.

''That was part of my life's education. Don't play a player, Lorrayne. Don't pretend that you're part of the established order when you're not.''

''I am a detective with the Aurora police department—''

He was losing ground and he knew it. He dug in harder. This was for Eric. ''That doesn't make you a robot.''

He was manipulating her, Rayne thought angrily. Or trying to. Which meant he was in for a surprise. Better men than he had tried to get her to do what they'd wanted and failed. ''That also doesn't make me an idiot.''

Impatience echoed in his voice. ''Never said you were.''

No, not in so many words, she thought, but he still underestimated her. ''But I'd be one if I let you just come in and use me to get your brother off.''

Cole sighed, struggling with his temper and wishing he had ordered a drink, a strong one. But he'd driven over here and the last thing he needed right now was to be pulled over and arrested for a DUI, which he could guarantee would happen if he downed the kind of drink he was thinking about.

"I don't want to use you, I need you. To get at the truth."

Everyone always said that, but they didn't mean it. What they wanted was for the truth to bear them out, to yield the kinds of answers they wanted to find. "Well, right now the truth of the matter is, the D.A. thinks they have your brother dead to rights for the murder of Kathleen Fallon."

He'd thought that she of all people'd know better. "You know how that works. Once they make an arrest, they stop looking around at anyone else and they start building a case."

"They *have* a case, Cole." She stopped. She'd never called him by his first name before. Her eyes narrowed. "I can call you Cole, can't I, seeing as how you're shouting at me?"

He made an effort to lower his voice and take some of the sarcasm out of it. "They have a *fabricated* case," he insisted.

As far as the police were concerned, the case seemed very solid. "Your brother's ring had Kathy's DNA on it, not to mention that it left a pretty damn good imprint on her face, right in the middle of a fractured cheekbone. His prints were all over her apartment. He was seen entering that evening. The neighbors heard them shouting. She had a restraining order against him—do you want me to go on?"

Cole recalled what Quinn's report had said. It looked pretty damning, but that didn't change the fact that he knew down to the core of his bones that Eric couldn't have done something like this. "He gave her that ring."

It was her turn to frown. "So what are you saying, she punched herself?"

He didn't appreciate being on the receiving end of sarcasm. The woman gave as good as she got. "No, but maybe she gave it to someone else and he used it on her."

She supposed the theory had some merit, but he was clearly reaching. She would have done the same if it were her brother facing prison for the rest of his life. "They do that on TV shows and in the movies. Usually life isn't that planned out."

His eyes held hers. "Usually. But that doesn't mean it couldn't have happened that way. Someone could have set him up to take the fall."

"So your theory is that an enemy set him up?"

"No, someone used him to cover up their part in the murder."

She blew out a breath. If anyone overheard them, she'd have some explaining to do. It was like telling tales out of school. "Look, I'm not supposed to be discussing this—"

"Why? As you said, it's not your case. That means you don't have a vested interest in keeping your mouth shut, Lorrayne."

She bristled. "My friends call me Rayne." Her meaning was clear. She didn't remotely consider him to be even close to that category. "You can call me Detective Cavanaugh."

She wasn't the kind to be bullied and he knew it. Though he hated doing it, he had no choice. She could very well be the key to unlocking this for him. He had no other options available right now. He threw himself on her mercy. "I will call you anything you want, just help me. My brother's being framed."

"Every family member wants to think that their brother, sister, mother, father, whoever, is innocent, but—"

He cut her off. "My parents don't."

Well, maybe that said it all, she thought. And Cole just didn't want to hear it. "They'd be in a position to know, wouldn't they? More than you."

Cole fought to keep his voice from rising again. "The woman at the perfume counter in Macy's department store knows more about my brother than they do. They were AWOL for most of Eric's life."

"And yours."

He hadn't come looking for her just to be drawn onto some imaginary couch and analyzed. "I'm not the one sitting in a jail cell."

For a large part of her life, she'd shied away from really opening up to people. She recognized a kindred behavior in someone else. Apparently, Cole Garrison shared her reverence for privacy. Ordinarily, she respected boundaries, but the growing passion in his voice had aroused her curiosity. "You really love your brother, don't you?"

Cole shrugged. The fact was a given, but not one he either voiced or debated. "He's my brother."

Her gaze never wavered. "That's not an answer,

that's just a point of biological fact. Plenty of brothers can't stand each other.'' She fell back, appropriately enough, on something she'd read in high school. ''If you remember your old English history, brothers have been known to kill one another.''

The woman had intelligent eyes. He could see she was constantly analyzing, dissecting, weighing. But that she had a taste for history surprised him. ''There's no throne of England at stake here. I'm all Eric has. I'm all he ever had. And I believe him when he says he didn't kill her.'' Cole leaned over the small table, pressing his case as his sense of urgency mounted. He needed to win her over. ''Look, Eric's a screwup, there's no denying that, but you knew him. He's harmless.''

She quickly picked up the word he'd used. ''You're right, I *knew* him,'' she emphasized. ''But I don't know him now. People change.'' Cole didn't have to look any farther than his mirror to know that. ''You did. You went from someone nobody thought would amount to anything and turned yourself into a businessman. Someone who does a lot of good without being asked or waits around to be acknowledged.'' She saw the questioning look in his eyes and couldn't help adding with a touch of smugness, ''I like to know who I'm being propositioned by.''

Maybe it was the softening lighting, or maybe it was the word she'd used, but something stirred within him as he looked at her face. Something that was completely out of sync with what they discussed.

''When I proposition you, you'll know,'' he promised her quietly, so quietly that she could almost feel the words whisper along her skin. "This isn't that time, Detective Cavanaugh. You're interested in justice, I'm interested in justice—"

It took her a second to pull herself together. "And if justice means sending your brother to prison for murdering Kathy Fallon—?"

"It won't. He didn't kill her." He was never more sure of anything in his life.

She fell back on the evidence again. "He stalked her. She had a restraining order against him. He was overheard threatening her—"

Cole shook his head. "He was drunk and hurt at the time."

She smiled at him as if he'd scored the winning point for her side. "Maybe he was drunk and hurt when he killed her. Maybe she drove him to it."

"Then we'll find that out, too, won't we?"

So he wasn't asking her to get rid of evidence or to whitewash his brother. Well, at least there was hope for him. But that still didn't change the situation she'd find herself in if she went at this full-tilt. And she wasn't about to tell Cole that she'd been quietly looking into the matter herself. He'd only seize on that.

"The police department doesn't like one of their own playing devil's advocate and questioning the findings of their own people."

The police department was no different from any other fraternal organization or company. But he didn't see her in a traditional role. "Since when did you ever live by the rules?"

Her eyes narrowed. She didn't like his assumptions, even if they were true. "For someone who didn't speak two words to me before today, you seem to think you know me pretty well."

He allowed himself a small smile as he recalled a far less complicated time. "You had a reputation around school. And, to be honest, I always thought we were kindred spirits."

That was a crock and they both knew it. Back then he'd been one of the cool kids just because of his don't-give-a-damn attitude. She'd just been considered someone on the fringe. "You wanted blue hair, too?"

She smiled then, slowly. He watched as a warmth filtered over her features.

"Inside," he clarified. "Kindred spirits inside." She wasn't the kind of person anyone could snow, so he went with the truth. "You wore clothes like a clown."

"And you looked like Darth Vader, dressed in black, dark and brooding." And sexy, she added silently. But she was sure he was already aware of that. "At least my hair's not blue anymore."

His eyes slid over her appreciatively. The clothes she'd used to favor had been baggy and had hidden the trim figure she now displayed. "Your taste in clothes has improved a great deal, as well."

She'd never liked the clothes she'd worn. She'd picked them out for a specific reason. "I wore those to annoy my father."

That she'd done what she'd done to rebel was something anyone could have understood. But he found himself wanting to know, for no earthly reason he could pinpoint, what had prompted her to be so blatantly rebellious. "Why?"

She shrugged. "I'm not sure anymore." She looked at him sharply. "And it doesn't have anything to do with the case."

"So you'll help?"

It wasn't that he was wearing her down, she was just curious what he thought she could accomplish. "Just what is it you want me to do?"

"Be a police detective. Go over the evidence they have, talk to the same people whoever's handling the case talked to—"

So far, he wasn't being illuminating. "You can pay a private investigator to do that."

He already had a private investigator. What he needed was something more. "You're on the inside. You're in a unique position—"

"Yes, to get my butt in a sling."

The thought of actually viewing something like that was not without its allure. But he wasn't here to be allured, he was here to try to save his brother the only way he knew how. "No, to make sure an innocent man isn't railroaded into going to prison for something he didn't do just because he was the wrong man in the right place."

She sighed. The tea had long since grown cold. She drank it anyway and then set down the small cup. "Are you going to talk until I say yes?"

He nodded. Words were all he had. He knew that, besides looking like a blatant bribe, offering her money in exchange for her services would have gotten him tossed out on his ear long ago. "Pretty much."

Her expression told him that he hadn't won yet. "You might wind up with a very dry throat."

"I'll risk it."

Something was happening here. Something she didn't entirely like or approve of. She could feel herself reacting to him and that was just wrong. On a lot of counts. It was time for some air. "Look, the best I can do is say I'll think about it."

"Fair enough."

She was sliding out of the booth. If he called for the check, he knew that by the time it arrived, the woman would be gone. Rising, he peeled off a hundred, far more than the two meals could have possibly approached, and left it on the table.

Surprising her, he took Rayne's arm and guided her toward the entrance. The restaurant was nearly filled to capacity. People began to line the bar, waiting for a table. It took them a couple of minutes to reach the door.

When they did, he helped her with her coat, slipping it onto her shoulders. "For how long?" he wanted to know. "How long do you need to think about it?"

With effort, she turned her face away from his and pushed open the door. She really needed that air now. She felt far too warm.

The air hit her with a blast. It felt good. Sobering. "Until I come to a conclusion."

Walking behind her, he wanted her to know something. "Any other time I'd back off, Detective, but we're fighting the clock here. Eric doesn't have very much time.'' She turned to face him. The wind had picked up since he'd gone inside. Cole slowly raised up her collar, his eyes never leaving her face. For an instant, a very foolish instant, he felt like kissing her. He didn't.

"Why don't you sleep on it and give me your answer in the morning?" he suggested. "I'm staying at Hyatt Regency. Room 1440."

She struggled not to let the shiver take possession of her body, telling herself it was only the cold, nothing more. "Not home?"

"Let's walk to your car." Not about to answer her, he took her arm and began to walk through the parking lot.

After a beat, she took the lead. "'I don't have a home here, Detective. And I doubt if I'm very welcome in my parents' home."

She stopped in the third row, beside her vehicle. Mist had gathered on its body and windshield. Rain was coming. "Why don't you try going to see them, anyway? People change."

There was an ironic twist to his lips. "Yes, some people get worse with time."

Taking out her key, she unlocked her door but didn't open it. "You're not any more upbeat now than you were then, are you?"

He shrugged, his shoulders moving beneath the tan coat. "I don't know about upbeat, but I'm more of a realist now than I was in high school."

"And you still believe your brother's innocent?" She supposed that meant something.

"I still believe my brother's innocent."

Opening the door, she slid in behind the steering wheel. "Okay."

He felt a nugget of hope being stirred. "You'll help Eric?"

He'd jumped to a conclusion and she was quick to set him straight. "No, okay I'll give you my answer in the morning."

He could accept that. He didn't have much of a choice. "All right, Detective Cavanaugh, until the morning, then."

She reached to close the door. "Oh, and you can call me Rayne."

"Does that mean we're friends?"

Unlike Teri and Clay, she didn't make friends quickly. That kind of thing was something she did slowly. After she was sure. "No, it just means that I don't have time to wait around until you finishing saying 'Detective Cavanaugh' every time you want to make a point."

He laughed softly, then closed the door for her. "See you in the morning, Rayne."

It wasn't until she'd pulled out of the lot that she realized he'd said "see" instead of merely "talk to you" in the morning. The man was nothing if not confident.

She, on the other hand, had a lot of issues to sort through.

Rayne laughed shortly to herself as she looked in

the rearview mirror before changing lanes. Who was she trying to kid? She'd already made up her mind before Cole Garrison had ever come on the scene. She'd started poking around in the case, not liking the direction it was headed. She was going to say yes to Cole. She just didn't like him assuming that she was complacent, or that he had that kind of sway over her, because he didn't. It was just the right thing to do.

Something about the case hadn't felt right to her from the start. She had nothing to point to but a gut hunch. Maybe it was because she had once gone out with Eric. Her feelings had changed over the years and all she felt now for Eric was sympathy. Even back then, beneath Eric's laughter and brassy manner, she'd felt there was a lost soul there. As lost as she was.

The only difference between them now was that she had managed to finally find her way out of the maze. Eric, apparently, had only managed to get himself deeper and deeper entrenched. But then, from what she'd ascertained and Cole had confirmed, Eric had never had the kind of support system she'd had. Her family had always been there for her to fall back on. The only person Eric ever had, had left town the day after his own high school graduation.

Was it guilt that had brought Cole back now?

She would have said that he wasn't the type to feel any guilt, but then, the same might have been said about her. She did feel guilty, very guilty over everything she'd put her family through, especially her father.

Odd how they kept seeming to have things in common, she thought as she drove home.

"Home early or just making a pit stop?"

Her father's voice floated to her, stopping Rayne in her tracks halfway across the foyer on her way to the stairs. Looking around, she saw him sitting in the living room, watching some program that obviously wasn't holding his attention. He had the sound on mute.

Rayne crossed to him and sat on the edge of the sofa arm. She glanced at the set. It was an old Clint Eastwood movie, one of the Dirty Harry ones, although she wasn't sure which one. Her father could have easily supplied the dialogue to all of them. Though he didn't always hold with "Harry's" methods, her father loved those movies.

"No, I'm home for the night."

Tossing the remote aside, he began to rise, only to have her push him back into his seat. "Did you eat?"

"All fed and diapered, Dad."

He snorted. "I'm not babying you. Adults have to eat, too."

"And if I'm hungry," she recited in a singsong voice, "I can fix myself something. I don't need you to wait on me."

"Never a waiter, more like a maître d'," he corrected. Then the humor faded from his face as he looked at her closely. "Anything I can help with?"

She could see his parenting radar going on fullblast. How did he *do* that? "What?" she asked warily.

"You've got that little groove between your eyes." He lightly ran the tip of his finger over it, as if to smooth it out. The groove only became deeper as she frowned at him. "The same one your mother used to get when she was busy trying to resolve something."

"I'm not trying to resolve anything."

Which only made Andrew smile. "She used to deny it, too."

Rayne sighed. There was no arguing with him when he was like this. Even so, she didn't want to get into a discussion about Cole Garrison, his brother Eric, or any of it, not tonight. Besides, she was fairly certain she knew what her father would have to say about her investigating on her own. He might have done it in his time, but it wasn't something he wanted any of his kids risking. The man clearly had a superhero complex. And maybe, just maybe, it had rubbed off a little on her. She wasn't just her mother's daughter, she was his, as well.

Rising, Rayne decided that maybe she needed a little time alone with the elliptical trainer in her room. "I'll let you know if I need a sounding board."

"Make sure you do," Andrew called after her as she went up the stairs.

Shaking his head, he sat back on the sofa and picked up his remote again. A block of commercials had been launched on the cable network and he began to surf around to see of there was anything worthwhile watching for the next three minutes or so.

He glanced at his watch. It was only seven-thirty, more than four hours earlier than the earliest time she normally came home after an evening out. Whatever she wrestled with had to be big.

He wondered if it had anything to do with what they'd talked about at the breakfast table. He supposed if she wanted him to know, she'd tell him.

But it was the waiting that drove him crazy.

With a sigh, he shut off the TV and got up. He wanted to reread the technician's findings with his wife's wallet again. Maybe there was something he'd missed earlier.

Chapter 5

She ran down a dark street that had no beginning, no end. She just knew she had to keep running and that eventually, she'd be safe. But not yet.

Not yet.

And then the ringing began. At first it sounded like a faraway church bell, declaring the hour. But as it continued, its timbre changed.

The ringing came closer, more persistent.

Layers of sleep pulled away until she became aware that the ringing came from beside her head.

Opening her eyes, Rayne saw the long, dark street melting away. The ringing didn't.

It was her phone.

With a shiver that chased away the last of her dream, Rayne groped around on the nightstand for the cell phone she'd left there.

''Hello?'' The word felt as if she'd gurgled it up. Rayne paused to clear the fog from her throat if not her brain and then repeated, ''Hello?''

''Did I wake you?''

She didn't immediately recognize the voice. Only a select few had her cell phone number and this didn't sound like any of them.

''No,'' she mumbled, ''I had to get up to answer the phone anyway.'' Up on her elbow now, Rayne dragged her hand through her hair, trying to pull herself together at the same time.

''Have you made up your mind yet?''

Now she recognized the voice. She sat up, awake as adrenaline poked its long, reedy fingers into her bloodstream. How the hell did he get her number? The man was becoming annoyingly resourceful.

''Garrison? What are you doing calling me?'' she demanded.

In contrast his voice was calm, patient. ''We had an arrangement.''

''Yes, but not one that began at—'' she paused to look at the clock that she'd pushed against her lamp in her search for the cell phone ''—six in the morning.''

''Sorry, I guess I'm still running on back east time.''

He didn't sound sorry, she thought, annoyed. He sounded sexy.

Rayne wiped away the thought. She didn't need this. ''Well, I'm not. Call back at a decent hour—after you've adjusted your clock.''

About to snap her phone shut and terminate the connection, she heard him say, "Rayne, please."

Swallowing an oath, she sighed. Something in his voice, other than the tone, stayed her hand. Maybe his sincerity spoke to her.

Or maybe her brain was still fogged over, she thought, annoyed with herself.

"All right." She didn't bother hiding her grudging reluctance. "I'll see what I can do to help you. But not at six in the morning. I'll talk to you later."

With that, she ended the call.

Punching her pillow into submission, Rayne tried desperately to get back to sleep. But the sound of his low and sexy voice refused to vacate her mind.

And when a half sleep finally began to descend on her, it only served to heighten her reaction to the man.

"Damn."

Giving up all attempts at a comforting sleep, Rayne laid on her back a moment longer, staring at the ceiling, the import of what she was about to undertake weighing heavily on her mind.

The only consoling fact was that she knew she wasn't doing it because of Cole. She was doing it because of Eric. And because something just didn't feel right to her about the case.

She couldn't put it in any better terms, even to herself. This didn't change the fact that when she'd heard of Eric Garrison's indictment for the murder of his former girlfriend, she'd first thought it was someone's poor idea of a joke. The Eric Garrison she'd known was too squeamish to kill a bug, much less a person. It had to be a mistake.

But when everyone seemed satisfied with the arrest, and when the body of evidence was put together, the D.A. felt they had a solid case, she knew everyone else took the notion seriously.

She still couldn't. And because it was someone she knew, she had to prove it to herself. Quietly, if possible. Without stepping on anyone's toes. She wasn't the reckless, the-hell-with-the-whole-world girl she'd once been, not giving a damn about herself or tomorrow. Now she knew she was part of an integral whole, that what she did affected others, most importantly, the people she loved.

But she still wanted answers.

With a sigh, and feeling half dead, she dragged herself upright in bed, swung her legs out and let them dangle over the side. Getting her bearings was hard, even under the best circumstances, and these weren't them. She'd never been one of those morning people, waking up eager to greet the day. She'd always met it reluctantly, her consciousness kicking and screaming as it was brought to the fore.

Today was no different.

Slowly the day of the week penetrated the layers of fog that still swirled around her brain. It was Saturday. Saturday, and she'd missed the opportunity to sleep in.

''Damn you, Cole Garrison,'' she said vehemently. He could have waited another hour for his answer.

A loud thud coming from the room next to hers

made her jump. If she'd still been asleep, the noise would have been enough to jar her awake. Because she was a Californian, born and bred, she automatically glanced at the light fixture overhead to see if it was swaying.

It wasn't.

That ruled out an earthquake, she thought. Another thud had her on her feet and quickly in the hallway, knocking on the door next to hers. "Everything okay in there?"

The next minute, the door opened. Clay stuck his head out, a sheepish grin playing on his lips. "Sorry, did I wake you?"

She peered into the room past his shoulder. There were boxes piled up everywhere. "Seeing as how I'm not dead, yes, you woke me. What the hell are you doing in here?"

He gestured toward the boxes. "Getting my gear together." He looked at her. "I'm moving out today, remember?"

"No," she snapped, then amended, "Yes." But that was a lie. She hadn't remembered. A vague piece of conversation around the table floated back to her, but it had no beginning or ending and she couldn't pin it down. "Maybe."

Shrugging her shoulders, Rayne took in a deep breath. She was still having trouble focusing. For once she wished she was like Teri. Clay's twin was like a spring in the morning, able to bounce up and just launch herself into the day no matter how little sleep she'd gotten the night before.

Crossing her arms in front of her, Rayne leaned against the doorjamb as her brother got back to work stowing his possessions into various boxes that were as yet unlabeled. If she knew Clay, they'd probably remain that way. A good detective, he wasn't the most organized of people in his personal life.

"Not that I don't love seeing you go, but what's the hurry?"

He laughed. Taking packing tape, he began to close up the box he'd just finished filling. "Now you sound like Dad."

She pretended to take offense. "No need to insult me, just answer the question. You're getting married soon, right?"

"Right." He took the last of his sweaters out of the bureau and deposited them in a tangled pile into the box. "Right after Callie and the good judge make it official."

Walking into the room, she elbowed him aside and began to fold his sweaters neatly. "So move out then." And then she realized what her formerly wild bachelor brother was probably up to. Her hands still busy, she looked at him knowingly. "Or is it that now that you and Ilene have gotten back together, you just can't contain yourself any longer?"

He waited until she finished before dumping the contents of his sock drawer on top of the folded sweaters. "That's none of your business," he said as he shoved the drawer back into the bureau. "I told Dad I'd move out the minute I found some place affordable."

She made the logical assumption. "And that would be Ilene's place." Rayne went to his closet. It was already empty. A pang nestled into her stomach. He'd moved back in just for a short while. That had stretched out to more than seven months. She was going to miss seeing him around. "Can't beat free, I guess."

Taking the tape, he began to seal another box. "For your information, I'm moving into a furnished apartment for the next two months."

She turned from the closet, surprised. "You're not moving in with Ilene?"

He shook his head. "Might send the wrong signals to Alex."

Ilene and Alex had stayed with them to ensure their safety before Ilene had gone on to give testimony about her company's sleight of hand in the annual stockholder's report. During that time, they had all fallen in love with the precocious boy.

"What? That his long-lost father is finally sleeping with his mother?"

Moving the box off the bed and next to the others he'd taped, Clay stopped packing for a moment.

"I've explained who I am to Alex and he's okay with it, but I don't want to dump too much on the boy at one time." Shrugging, he resumed dividing the sum total of his possessions amid the remaining boxes. "It's better this way."

She sat on the corner of the bed. "Maybe for you, but I'm not too sure about Dad. He's going to miss having another male around the place." It had taken her a while, but she was finally beginning to appreciate life from her father's side of the fence. "One by one, his birds are leaving the nest." She looked at Clay. "Leaving him more time to pore over Mom's file."

Their father's preoccupation with what they felt was a hopeless quest had been a source of concern for all of them.

Clay offered his suggestion tongue-in-cheek—for the most part. "Then maybe you and Teri can take turns not being out until all hours and keep him company."

She gave him a dirty look. Getting off his bed, she started emptying the small bookcase that held his tapes and books. "Here, let me give you a hand with all that. Maybe we can have you out before noon."

Laughing, Clay threw his treasured Angel cap at her. It's been the one he'd worn the time the team had had the all-important rally in the seventh inning of the sixth World Series game. She caught it, then ran out of the room, challenging him to catch her.

And missing him already.

Cole couldn't sit still, couldn't just wait for Rayne to call him back. He had to do something. Every minute was precious. Every minute that wasn't used was another that brought Eric closer to a verdict he didn't deserve, one that would lock him away from a life he hadn't mastered, sending him to a place akin to hell. Cole had no delusions about his brother. Eric was the type who had "victim" clearly printed on his forehead. Once in general lockup with hardened criminals,

Eric wouldn't last out the month. He wouldn't be able to survive mixed in with those kinds of people.

Making up his mind, Cole went back to jail. He went with the intent of getting as much information out of his brother as possible, starting with the names of some of the people who had been at the party he'd attended.

Sitting opposite him, Eric made vague responses, not out of any sense of loyalty to the people who had been there, but because he really couldn't remember.

"I gave all those names to the police already," he protested. "The ones I could remember. Most of it's kind of hazy," he'd confessed, then added, "I guess most of my life's been kind of hazy lately. Ever since you left, really." And then, looking afraid that he'd sent the wrong message, he quickly added, "Hey, man, I don't mean to dump that on you. It's not your fault. You got out. I'm glad for you. Me, I never had enough guts to try." Eric sighed like a man who knew all of his limitations and was powerless to do anything about them. "I liked being close to the purse strings too much. Not that it matters anymore." Those strings had been tightened and the money cut off less than a month ago. His reserve was almost gone.

Eric's expression was sheepish as he looked at him and asked for understanding. "I'm not like you, Cole. I never got a backbone."

Pity mingled with sympathy. Eric was such a tangled mess, he didn't know where to begin to make it right. But making excuses wasn't the way to resolve anything. "They're standard issue at birth."

Eric laughed shortly, staring at the tips of his fingers as he rested his hands on the table in front of him. "My order got botched." He raised his eyes to Cole's face. "But that was why I loved Kathy. With her, I felt different, as if I could do things. She made everything clear, everything in focus." His face fell as he struggled with a memory. "When she told me she didn't want to see me anymore, it ripped my heart right out of my chest.

"That's why I kept at her, Cole. I was trying to win her back. I wouldn't have hurt her. Kathy was the only thing that made life worth living. I knew it couldn't be about the money. She hadn't been with me because of the money." It was almost a plea for agreement. Tears shimmered in his eyes again. "I never felt about anyone the way I did about her. You know what I mean?"

No, Cole thought, he didn't. He'd never loved anyone, never felt that tightening in the gut he'd heard about. His emotions had all been frozen years ago. "Not firsthand, but yeah, I know what you mean."

The guard entered the room. "Time's up."

Cole nodded, rising. He saw Eric flinch as the latter got to his feet. The handcuffs returned. His brother looked at him with supplicating eyes. "Get me out of here, Cole. Please."

The words still rang in his ears as he drove up the familiar winding path that brought him to the mansion. He'd come against his better judgment, come not because he wanted to see them after ten years, but because they were where the money was. At least they could be good for that. God knew they hadn't been good for anything else.

They hadn't aged any.

It was the first thought that occurred to him when, walking behind a maid he didn't recognize, he was brought into the secondary living room. Fifty years ago the room might have been called a parlor, a place where guests who belonged to the B-list of acquaintances were politely received.

Unlike Eric, whose lifestyle had embedded itself on his face, making his brother look years older than he was, his parents looked as if not a day had gone by since he'd last seen them.

"We hear you're doing very well, Cole," his father said after the obligatory words of greeting had been gotten out of the way.

Cole looked from one parent to the other. His mother resembled an old painting, demurely posed. His father was the personification of old money. Not a single true emotion between the two of them.

"I can't complain," he finally answered.

And then his father smiled at him. Cole was hard-pressed to remember if he had ever seen the expression on his father's face within this house. There had been plenty of instances when a smiling face had looked up at him from the society papers, but he didn't recall ever seeing it in person.

"Well, we're proud of you," his father said heartily.

The words of praise, of approval, left him cold. The

last time Cole had wanted either from one of his parents, he'd been eight years old. Trying to get his father's attention after some accomplishment, he'd been shunted to the side.

Any further chitchat would just be perpetrating a lie. These people had never cared about him and he no longer cared about them. Eric's plight was the reason he was here, so he got down to the heart of the matter.

"I'm here about Eric."

The smile vanished as if it had only been a figment of his imagination. His father's still-handsome face frosted over. "Who we are definitely *not* proud of."

Cole watched his mother knot her fingers together as she sat ramrod-straight on the Louis XIV chair she'd lavished more attention on than either one of her children.

He wasn't here to debate that, or to point out that had they not failed as parents, maybe they would have had a son to be proud of.

"You can still bail him out of jail until the trial."

His father looked at him as if he'd just been asked to disrobe and run naked through the center of the city. "Why should we do that?"

No, he wasn't devoid of emotion, Cole thought, because he felt anger welling up inside of him. He had an almost uncontrollable urge to shout at this man who had sired him. He didn't waste his time or his breath to say that he believed Eric was innocent. If they'd had bothered to get to know his brother, they would have known that already.

His voice was steely as he said, ''Because he's your son.''

His father eyed the liquor cabinet. It was an open secret that Lyle Garrison lubricated his brain cells with healthy doses of liquid libation. Eric had inherited his father's penchant for drinking. That he did it indiscriminately and habitually wound up drunk was probably one of the reasons his father disliked his second born so much.

''He's brought nothing but shame to the family name. He should be grateful that we're providing legal counsel for him.''

Cole couldn't restrain himself any longer. ''Maybe if you and Mother—'' he spared her a damning glance ''—had provided something more when Eric was growing up, you wouldn't have anything to be ashamed of right now.''

His father turned a very unflattering shade of red as rage snapped into place. ''Oh, so now it's our fault? Oh, that's right, Denise, did you know that it's fashionable to blame the parents any time you screw up?''

''Never mind that the parents screwed up first,'' Cole pointed out.

Lyle Garrison drew himself up to his full height. Men who towered over him quaked in his presence because he had the power and the money to break them into small pieces. It seemed to gall him that his son didn't shrink back. ''What are you saying?''

Cole remained unaffected and he knew it goaded his father no end. ''What should have been said a long time ago. That if there were two people who were definitely *not* meant to be parents, it's you and Mother.'' Disgust filled his eyes as he looked from one to the other. ''There's not a drop of compassion, of kindness, within either of you.''

His father's voice fairly shook with barely suppressed rage. ''Well, this is some reunion, I must say. Did you come here to insult us?''

Eric, think of Eric, Cole counseled himself. ''No, I came to ask you get Eric out of jail. Being there is killing him.''

His mother finally broke her silence. ''And having this scandal dropped on our doorstep is killing me. Did he ever stop to think of that before he…did what he did?''

His father looked at him contemptuously, although he kept his distance, as if sensing that he would not come out the winner in a confrontation with his son. ''If you're so concerned about him, Cole, why don't *you* bail him out?''

If the bail hadn't been set as high as it was, he would have had Eric out the moment he'd arrived in Aurora. But his money was all tied up in his latest project and there wasn't enough cash to use. ''I don't have enough collateral to put up. But you do.''

Taking out a decanter, his father poured brandy into a goblet. Cole caught the slight look of dismay filter over his mother's face, but she said nothing. She never opposed his father.

''If that's the only reason you're here, Cole,'' his father said before he raised the glass to his lips, ''I don't see as how we have anything else to talk about.''

"I guess not." He was an idiot to have come here. An idiot to have thought that there was an ounce of compassion to be squeezed out of either of them. "Mother, Dad—" he nodded at each "—nice seeing you both again. Don't bother getting up, I'll see myself out." Sarcasm reeked from his words as he strode out of the room and then out of the house.

He slammed the front door in his wake as he left.

Time had mellowed him somewhat. He didn't lose his temper anymore, certainly not like that, but dealing with his bloodless parents got to him. He'd gone to them against his better judgment. What was worse, he'd failed.

Cole was still not in the best frame of mind when he strode into the hotel. He'd noticed the speedometer inching its way up to seventy as he'd driven back. It echoed the way he felt, as if he was in danger of reaching a maximum boiling point. Getting his temper under control took some doing.

He was halfway across the hotel's elegantly carpeted floor when a bellhop, hurrying behind him, tapped him on the shoulder. "Mr. Garrison?"

Swinging around, he barked, "Yes?" then amended, "Sorry. Anything I can do for you?"

The bellhop looked at him sheepishly. "The lady asked me to tell you to meet her in the hotel restaurant when you came in."

Cole looked around the lobby, but saw no one he recognized. "What lady?"

"This one." The bellhop produced a business card and handed it to him.

Cole found himself looking down at Rayne's name. Was this a good sign? Or had she come down in person to give him bad news?

He was getting ahead of himself. There was no reason to surmise that there was any bad news to give. Seeing his parents again had brought out all the worst emotions within him.

"And the restaurant would be…?"

"Right that way, sir." The bellhop pointed toward the left. Upon entering the hotel, Cole had been vaguely aware of an opening leading off to a darkened area. He hadn't bothered to read the sign on the wall to learn that he was passing the hotel's finer restaurant. Food hadn't been on his mind.

"Thanks." He tipped the bellhop and crossed to the restaurant.

It took him a moment to acclimate his eyes to the lighting, which was subdued and warm and made him think of velvet. Standing in the doorway, he scanned the interior. He saw her just as the hostess walked up to him. Waving the woman back, he strode into the restaurant and toward Rayne's table.

"Good or bad?" he asked.

"Excuse me?"

She'd taken her eyes off the entrance for just a moment. Wouldn't you know he'd pick that time to walk in? She didn't like being caught off guard. Neither did she like enigmatic questions.

He seated himself at the table. The last arrangement

they'd made, she was to call him. He hadn't expected her to just show up. The way his morning had gone, he didn't feel very hopeful.

"Is it good news or bad that brings you here? Because I have to warn you, if it's bad, you might want to hold off telling me," Cole barked. The hostess had followed him and now placed a menu in front of him. A perfunctory smile came and left his lips. His attention remained on Rayne. "Never mind, disregard that. I need to know, even if it's bad."

Rayne waited until he finally paused. "Is this a private conversation or can anyone leap in at will?"

"Sorry. Speak."

She frowned. "Now that's one of the things we're going to have to get out of the way."

He had little patience with riddles. "What are you talking about?"

"You ordering me around. If you want my help, we do things my way or no way," she told him simply.

Fresh from a visit to a megalomaniac, Cole could feel his antennae going up. "I don't think I like the sound of that."

"There's not going to be another sound, at least, not from me, unless you agree to my terms."

He'd never reacted well to being given ultimatums. "And if I don't?"

She picked up her purse. "Then I'm afraid I've just wasted my time."

His nerves were on edge. Maybe he was overreacting. Besides, this wasn't about him, it was about saving Eric. "Hold on, I said if, remember?"

She was slow to relent. A good part of her still didn't think this was such a good idea, allowing him to throw in his lot with hers. She moved better and faster on her own. There was less chance of having anyone else find out that she was conducting her own investigation if she was the only one involved. "Then you agree? We do things my way?"

He'd learned how to delegate in his business, but it was something he still had to master privately. This would be the place to begin. "As long as it gets results—fast—" he emphasized, "I'll agree to anything."

Anything, huh? She couldn't help the smile that rose to her lips. "Lucky for you I'm not the type to hold you to something like that. Never leave yourself open that way."

"I'll take it under advisement. So it's a deal?" He put out his hand.

After a beat she placed hers into it. "The 'deal' is we both want justice, leave it at that."

"Whatever you say."

She doubted that he meant that, but she intended to hold him to it when the time came. She had a feeling that it would be fairly soon.

Rayne picked up the menu. "Okay," she agreed gamely as she opened the menu, "then lunch is on you."

Chapter 6

Her father had always taught her that the best approach was the direct one. It saved time, let people know exactly where you stood and often caught them off guard. Enough to make it work in your favor. The element of surprise, she'd learned, was not to be underestimated. People had a tendency to blurt things out when they weren't prepared.

The following Monday, Rayne kept her father's lesson in mind and went straight to the horse's mouth—the officer who'd first found the body, a man she'd known from her very first days on the force.

When she cornered the tall, thin officer on the first floor of the police station, Richard Longwell apparently thought it might be for a different reason than the case.

His ready smile of greeting faded as he listened to

Rayne ask who had first discovered Kathy Fallon's body. A look of mild confusion flared in his brown eyes. Rayne wondered if she didn't pick up just a bit of hostility, as well.

Taking off his hat, Longwell ran a hand through his unruly dark brown hair.

"A girlfriend called it in. She and Kathy worked together at a boutique downtown. When Kathy didn't show, or answer her phone, the girlfriend came over to see what was going on. Kathy had told her that she was afraid Garrison might try something. There was no answer when she knocked, but the lights were still on. The girlfriend had someone from the housing complex open the door. She saw the body and called 9-1-1 " He shrugged. "I was the closest to the scene. She said she didn't touch anything. All that blood freaked her out."

Though the scene mentally filled her with horror, Rayne had learned from the very first to put distance between any personal reaction and what she saw on the job. She wouldn't have been able to be of any use otherwise. "And?"

Longwell shook his head. "She'd been stabbed. The M.E. said it happened the night before. Pretty little thing. She wasn't so pretty when Garrison—the suspect," he corrected with obvious sarcasm, "got through with her. There were signs of struggle. Garrison's prints were all over the place." His eyes narrowed as he looked at her. "Look, I put all that down in my report. Told the same to Rollins and Webber who caught the case. Why do you want to know? You haven't gone I.A.B. on me, have you, Cavanaugh?''

There was only a hint of humor in the man's voice. She and Longwell had attended the police academy together. They had even gone out a few times but they were in different places at the time. He was content to let his career progress in slow motion while from the first Rayne had been determined to arrive at a higher level. She'd been more driven than most people, but then, most people in the department hadn't had a Cavanaugh legacy to fulfill. Which was why she was now a detective while Longwell was still a patrolman.

They'd drifted apart in the last year and there were times she felt, despite what he said, that Longwell resented the fact that she outranked him now. But then again, that could have just been the pessimistic way she tended to view things.

That he thought she might have become part of the Internal Affairs Bureau, a self-policing branch of the force that everyone else distrusted and despised, stung. Even so, the irony that she had taken it upon herself to reexamine another policeman's findings was not lost on her.

''You know better than that.'' Her tone was a bit sharper than she'd intended.

Longwell's easy, charming smile returned as he held his hands up in front of him. ''Hey, easy now. Just curious why you seem so interested in the case.''

She could tell him the truth about that without any concern. ''I knew Eric Garrison once. Went to school with him.''

"Back during your wild past?" He hooked one thumb on his belt. His eyes passed over her a bit freely. "Date him, too?"

That was the problem with having so many members of her family on the force. It was hard to keep anything a secret. Not that her less than sterling past was something that could remain buried. Too many people had known her back then. And pitied Andrew Cavanaugh that his youngest had turned out to be such a handful and a half.

Her eyes met Longwell's and held steady. "As a matter of fact, I did. Once or twice."

A hint of a smirk crossed his small mouth. "Looks like not everyone you went out with turned out to be harmless."

If he only knew the half of it, Rayne thought. She'd gone out with men who would have turned her father's hair white, not gray, if he'd known. Her mouth curved slightly as she cocked her head, still looking at Longwell. "Present company excluded?"

The charming smile was back. "Goes without saying." And then it faded just a shade. "Seriously, why *are* you asking? Something strike you as off?

She hadn't gone deep enough into it to be able to actually point to anything beyond her gut feeling. She lowered her voice as a couple of patrol officers walked by them. "I just don't think he's capable of killing someone."

The laugh was cool, knowing. "Everyone's capable of killing, just have to press the right buttons. Were you out the day they taught that?"

"Apparently."

She knew she wasn't going to get anything further out of Longwell, at least, not at this time. Friends or not, police officers were a tight, fraternal group, not ready to speak out of turn unless there was bad blood involved. And as far as she knew, no one had done Longwell a bad turn.

"Thanks for your time," she murmured, walking away.

She could feel Longwell's eyes following her all the way down the hall.

This wasn't going to get her anywhere, Rayne thought at the end of the day. There was really no way she could work her cases with Joel Patterson, her partner, and get anywhere verifying the information that was involved in the case against Eric. Spread too thin, she wasn't going to be any use to anyone.

Something was going to have to give.

Rather than head out the door, she went in the opposite direction. Toward Lieutenant Gil MacLeroy's glass-enclosed office. He was alone.

Knocking once, she stuck her head into the office. "Do you have a minute?"

He was clearly a man on his way somewhere. Pausing, the lieutenant looked at his watch. "I can give you forty-five seconds."

"I'll talk fast."

"Never doubted it for a moment." He sat back down. "What's on your mind?"

"I need to take some time off."

"You're putting in for personal time?" His graying, tufted eyebrows rose high upon his broad forehead, accentuating just how really bald the man was. "Is this a first?"

"Yes, Sir, it is."

She hadn't put in for any time since she'd gotten on the force, nor taken any vacation days. Beyond an occasional few hours here and there, necessitated usually by some kind of family business, she was almost a permanent fixture in the department. Her dedication wasn't a matter of her being a workaholic. She had something to prove, to herself and to her family. It took a lot to live down a reputation that was less than glowing and she knew she was going to have to put in a great deal of time and effort to bury it.

Placing the tips of his fingers together, MacLeroy studied her intently for a moment.

Rayne couldn't help wondering if he suspected the reason behind her request. But if he meant to drag a confession out of her, he was going to be disappointed. She returned the lieutenant's gaze unflinchingly. She'd been called out on the carpet by the best, so she could well hold her own. Compared to her father, MacLeroy was a pussycat.

He shook his head doubtfully. "We're pretty busy right now."

Not any more than usual. She'd checked around the squad room this afternoon. "With all due respect, Sir, we're always busy."

He inclined his head, conceding the point with reluctance. It was a well-known fact that he liked a full complement of detectives on hand at all times. "How much time do you need?"

She thought of the upcoming trial. It was set for the following Tuesday. "A week."

The lieutenant glanced toward the large calendar on his desk. "I guess we can spare you for a week." His smile was one meant to put a subordinate at ease. "Where are you going?"

She hadn't moved a muscle since she'd entered his office. "Excuse me?"

"On vacation, where are you going?"

Because her teens had been so fraught with lies and deception, to the point that she herself began to lose the thread of what was real and what wasn't, these days, whenever possible, she tried very hard not to lie. Besides, saying she was going off to some vacation paradise might prove problematic if she needed to come into the precinct.

"Nowhere," she told him. "I just have to take care of some things."

MacLeroy accepted the explanation. "So we can be in touch if we need you?"

She grinned, relieved. "Absolutely."

"All right, it's settled. Just let Patterson know," he reminded her. "See you in a week."

She murmured goodbye, then went back to her desk to write a quick note to her partner, who'd left before her. As she lay down her pen, she saw Patterson walking back in. Obviously he hadn't gone for the day the way she'd hoped. "I was just leaving you a note."

Looking neither surprised nor curious, Patterson, a

twenty-seven-year veteran of the force, asked in a weary voice, "About?"

Rather than answer, she handed him the note. He scanned it quickly, then tossed the note out. Patterson looked rumpled. Going beyond just the state of his clothes, it was a deep-seated rumpled that took in every part of him. He made no secret of the fact that he didn't care for being paired with someone half his age. They'd been paired together for less than six months. He still viewed her as an annoying anomaly.

The man shrugged his broad, beefy shoulders beneath a tan jacket that looked slept in. "Suit yourself."

"Thanks, I will."

If pride hadn't prevented it, she would have asked for a change in partners. But that would have been the childish way and she was determined to tough things out. The last thing she wanted was for word to get back to her father that she couldn't cut it. She was determined to prove otherwise. She could handle anything the department had to throw at her.

It was what life had thrown at her that had been difficult for her to handle. But she had finally come to terms with that, as well. She wasn't the only girl who'd lost her mother and her loss, even though it made no sense to her, she had to accept and move on with her life.

Execution took some doing, but she was finally in the home stretch.

Sunset had long since come and gone by the time she got into her car. She sighed as she closed the door and then buckled up. Then sighed louder as she heard her cell phone ring. Her phone was in her back pocket, not easily gotten to once her seat belt was in place.

Muttering under her breath, she unbuckled again and then reached for her phone. It took effort to keep the impatience out of her voice.

"Cavanaugh," she sighed.

"Back off."

Annoyance gave way to adrenaline. Habit had her looking around, but the half-empty parking lot was unpopulated. "What? Who is this?"

"Back off," the voice repeated. The next moment the connection broke.

Biting off a curse, she opened her door to let in more light as she angled her phone's LCD screen. No number registered. The only thing that appeared was the word "private."

Most likely, it was a prank. Or a wrong number, but even as she manufactured excuses, Rayne couldn't shake the eerie feeling that clung to her.

She put the cell phone back in her pocket. Was it someone on the force? Had Longwell talked to someone about what she'd asked him? Someone who didn't want their toes walked on?

Or were more than toes at stake here? Did someone not want her digging in because the wrong man really was in prison?

Her mind turned to Cole.

What if he'd been the one who'd just placed that call to her? He had her cell number. Maybe asking her to investigate was just a ruse to throw her off, to make her predisposed into thinking that Eric hadn't murdered Kathy Fallon when he actually had? The call could have been made to make her think someone didn't want her finding out the truth.

Her head began to hurt from all the colliding theories.

"Stop it, Rayne," she chided herself. "Work with the evidence, not with some half-formed theories."

For the time being she went with the thought that someone was getting nervous. Which meant that she was right from the start.

She needed to talk to Cole.

Instead of going home, she drove to his hotel.

Cole Garrison had a room on the fourteenth floor. Suites were located on the seventeenth. Riding up, she wondered why he hadn't booked himself a suite. From what she'd gleaned, the man could well afford it.

He didn't answer when she knocked. Giving him to the count of ten, she knocked again, harder this time. There was still no response. Debating between going for the desk clerk or just opening the door herself, a trick she'd picked up from someone who'd worked summers at the hotel, she found she had to do neither.

The door finally opened.

"It's about time. Where were you?" she asked as she strode in. Turning around to face him, she came to a dead stop.

He was wet, dripping and dressed in only a towel. A relatively small towel, given the length of his body.

Damn.

It was the first word that echoed in her head, silently

uttered in sheer admiration for the upper torso on display.

Rayne had no idea that he was so sculpted beneath his finely tailored suit, although his broad shoulders had clearly hinted at it.

It took her a very long, very hot second to find her tongue. Her words felt all stuck together when they finally emerged. "Most people shower in the morning."

His towel was in danger of going south at any second. Cole secured it as best he could, keeping one hand over the point where the ends joined together. He wondered if she knew that the look in her eyes was flattering. And stirring. "Most people don't have a waiter spill Rigatoni Alfredo in their lap."

"Ouch." She winced in utter sympathy, her eyes traveling down to the area in question before zipping back up again as she realized what she was doing. "No damage done, I trust."

Was that a pink hue to her cheek or just a trick of the light? Had to be the latter. He doubted if anything could make Rayne Cavanaugh blush.

"Only to the suit." She obviously had something on her mind. He nodded toward the bathroom. "Mind if I get dressed?"

When he moved, his muscles rippled. Rayne cleared her throat. "Actually, I'd prefer it."

She heard him laugh as he walked back into the bathroom, closing the door behind him. Something burned within her, whether in reaction to his laugh or his very firm, spectacular body, she didn't know. It didn't matter. The flames had to be smothered either way.

In an effort to distract herself, she looked around the hotel room. There was just the single room, not unlike hundreds of others within the hotel. The room didn't befit a man whose parents could have bought and sold Rhode Island twice over.

She raised her voice to be heard through the bathroom door. "I thought you were doing well."

"I am."

"This isn't a very fancy room." Without question, his brother would have demanded the best the hotel had on hand.

"I don't require all that much. I don't believe in throwing money away on trappings I don't need."

"Except for the Porsche," she said.

There was humor in his voice when he echoed, "'Except for the Porsche." The bathroom door opened.

His hair still damp, he came out wearing a pullover blue sweater and jeans. A puff of warmth followed him. Cole was still barefoot and she found she had to work hard at not letting her thoughts drift back to the way he'd looked in his towel.

Wine wasn't the only thing that got better with age, she thought.

Because she felt he could read her mind, she gestured around the room. "Is that in rebellion against your parents?"

The smile on his lips was self-deprecating. Or perhaps just amused. "I'm almost twenty-nine years old.

I'm too old to rebel for rebellion sake." He'd never particularly welcomed thoughts or conversations about his parents, now more than ever. "I always thought they just possessed things to make up for how empty and shallow they really were."

"I take it that your first meeting with them didn't exactly go well," Rayne said.

He poured himself a drink from the bar. Something told him he might need one. "How did you know I went to see them?"

"I didn't." When he silently raised a glass in her direction, she shook her head. If there was one thing she desperately needed right now it was a clear head. Cole's near naked image refused to vacate her brain. Alcohol would only make it more vivid. "I took a guess. Eric's in jail and you can't bail him out, but they can. I figured you'd go to see them."

He'd called his lawyer to see if there was any way he could put up his business to raise the money, but most of his funds were in escrow pending the completion of his latest project. It was a formality, but right now, a damn inconvenient one.

He took a taste of his drink, then set it down. "So, did any of your powers of deduction get anywhere today where it counts?"

"I talked to Longwell—the first officer on the scene," Rayne added in case he wasn't familiar with the name.

"I know who Longwell is," he told her patiently. Sitting on the bed, he gestured for her to take a seat.

She did, choosing the single chair at the table. It

seemed somehow safer that way. "Did your homework?"

"I found out everything I could before I came to you," he informed her.

It was time to get down to the reason she was here. His close to all-natural appearance earlier had almost thrown it completely out of her head. She watched his eyes as she said, "Here's something you might not know. Someone called me on my cell phone just as I was leaving the station."

He got the feeling she was leaving something unsaid. Like an accusation. Impatience flared up, coming out of nowhere. He got up again, leaving his drink on the nightstand.

"You're right. I didn't know that." Cole ran his fingers through his hair before picking up a hair dryer. But rather than use it, he met her eyes in the mirror. "Is there a point to this?"

Because it was hard to see his eyes from her vantage point, she moved to stand next to him, staring up into his face. "The point is that whoever was on the line told me to back off."

"Back off?"

"Back off," she repeated.

He frowned, putting the dryer down. "What else did he say?"

"Just that."

"No threat beyond that?"

"It was implied." He'd looked properly surprised, but it could all be an act. "You don't know anything about that, then?"

He turned from the mirror, their bodies inches apart, his challenging hers. "Why would I know anything about that phone call? What are you saying, Rayne? Why would I threaten you?"

"To get me more interested."

It took him a second to follow her reasoning and even then, it didn't make sense. But neither did having Eric sit in jail, accused of murder. "So you work like that? The complete opposite of what's asked of you? The Eve syndrome? Forbidden fruit turn you on?"

She looked at him long and hard.

Yes, whispered through her brain as she felt every nerve ending stand at attention. *When the forbidden fruit looks like you.*

It was a credit to her self-control as well as her talents for performance that she said, "Not particularly. But getting at the truth does."

Turning away, he switched on the dryer and passed it over his semidry hair. Instead of a brush or a comb, he used his fingers.

"Sounds to me as if someone doesn't want you to get at the truth."

She raised her voice to be heard above the hair dryer. "Or someone wants me to think that someone doesn't want me to get at the truth."

"I'm sorry, I don't do riddles. But if you think I called you, have the phone records checked out." Finished, he put down the hair dryer and plucked his cell phone out of his back pocket. He handed the silver half-shell to her. "Mine. The hotel's."

There was a third, more likely possibility. "You could have placed the call from a public phone."

She made no effort to take the phone from him. He tucked it back into his pocket. "Well, that makes things harder now, doesn't it? You'll just have to take my word for it. I was too busy talking to Eric's ex-girlfriends, or at least scratching the surface of that very large, inharmonious group, to call you up and do heavy breathing." Cole was beginning to think his brother needed some serious help when it came to selecting the right type of woman. He'd run across nothing but gold diggers and airheads so far.

"No heavy breathing," she contradicted. "Just two words. Said twice."

His eyes met hers and held for a long moment. He hadn't a clue what was going on in her mind, but it didn't take much to know that she didn't exactly think of him as an ex-Boy Scout. Few people did. Only the ones whom he'd managed to place into houses, making their impossible dreams come true.

"I guess you'll just have to trust me on this, then. I didn't call you and, before you ask, I didn't have anyone else call you, either." Cole appealed to her sense of logic. "My brother is going to be on trial for his life unless I find out something to save him. I don't have any time to play games, Rayne. Now you can believe me or not, the choice is yours, but I can't make it any plainer than that."

She studied him for a very long moment. She wasn't one to give her trust easily. Of all of her siblings, she'd always been the most cautious, the most suspicious.

But something about the expression on Cole Garrison's face, the look in his eyes, negated any distrust she naturally felt.

"All right," she conceded, "I believe you."

Chapter 7

He looked at her for a long moment. Rayne had absolutely no way to gauge what he was thinking. The man would make an excellent poker player. Something her cousin Janelle could appreciate.

She, however, was given to more than her share of impatience. She liked having answers, not questions and this man raised more than his share of the latter without yielding any of the former.

"Good," he finally said. "Trust is the cornerstone of everything else. Let's move forward."

She was still trying to find her way here. The fact that Cole still smelled of soap and her mind was still fresh with the impression of his dripping, near nude body wasn't helping to keep her brain at its sharpest. "Excuse me?"

"Move forward," he repeated. He was hoping for

more, for some bombshell of a discovery that would blow the door off Eric's cell and set his brother free. When she didn't say anything, his eyes narrowed as he studied her. "You didn't come to my hotel room just to ask me if I'd called you on your cell phone and done a bad imitation of Darth Vader, did you?"

And get one hell of an eyeful, Rayne added silently, though she maintained an impassive expression on her face. "Actually, I did. And as for the voice, it wasn't as deep as Darth Vader's. Just male." That wasn't strictly a nondisputed fact. "Actually, I'm not even sure about that," she admitted.

"Voice synthesizer?"

She shook her head. "Whisper. Whoever called me on my cell whispered. Could have been a female, now that I think of it. Some women have deep voices."

Rayne had a deep voice, he thought. Just deep enough to slide effortlessly under a man's skin. His eyes held hers. "Like warm bourbon being poured down the side of a glass on a cold day."

The look in his eyes was doing it again, causing earthquakes in heretofore peaceful regions. Rayne took in a long breath. There was no getting away from it, something was definitely going on here between the two of them, something she couldn't—wouldn't—put a label on. But that didn't make it disappear.

"Something like that," she murmured.

He didn't bother hiding his disappointment. Granted he'd approached her on Friday and this was only Monday, but still, he'd expected her to come through with some sort of tidbit, some kind of insight in that time. "And that's it?"

Why did she suddenly feel like a gifted child who had uttered the wrong last letter in a national spelling bee contest? She hadn't failed, not yet. It was too soon to fail.

Too soon was a relative term, she reminded herself. In this case, Eric Garrison didn't have all that much time before too soon became too late.

However, that didn't change the fact that she didn't have anything new to offer his brother. "No earth-shaking revelations, if that's what you mean. The only inside track I have is to paperwork I'm sure you've already gotten your hands on nefariously." The items in the evidence room had been no less enlightening. So far, she had to admit that the case was stacking up against Eric. And yet when she'd read the autopsy report she'd come away with a nagging feeling there was something she was missing.

He shoved his hands into his pockets. "You mean, the official police report."

So far she'd only been able to get her hands on the first part of the report. Longwell wasn't an eager beaver, but he was good about filing his paperwork. "I took a look at Officer Longwell's statement. No surprises there. As for Rollins and Webber—" she shrugged vaguely to hide her frustration "—neither one takes too kindly to having someone looking over their shoulder. They're kind of like my partner that way."

He was surprised by her admission. He'd thought

that all police partners were supposed to present uni-
fied fronts to the public and one another. "Your partner doesn't like you looking over his shoulder?"

Patterson hadn't gone out of his way to hide the
fact that he felt saddled with her. She knew that he
was waiting for her to fail ignobly. The fact that she
did well only seemed to irritate him further.

She laughed dryly. "My partner doesn't like anyone
who can't remember the Vietnam war from firsthand
experience."

"You don't get along."

Because she was determined to do well and not give
her father any cause to be ashamed of her, she kept
her tongue in check whenever Patterson directed a
snide comment in her direction.

"Let's just say we have a tentative truce. I'm sure
if I put in for a transfer tomorrow, Patterson wouldn't
shed any tears. He thinks I am where I am because of
my name."

He could see how that ticked her off. Not that he
blamed her. "Are you?"

A dangerous light shone in her eyes as she looked
at him. He found himself amused as only someone in
the same boat could have been.

"The only thing my name ever did for me was put
unnaturally high expectations on my performance. Being a Cavanaugh doesn't open doors, it gets you an
audience, people watching, waiting to see if you mess
up."

"Not easy living with a name, is it?"

She opened her mouth, then shut it again, realizing

that, by the look on his face, she'd stumbled across something else they had in common. "You'd be the one to know, wouldn't you?"

He laughed shortly. "Firsthand." But that was where their similarities ended. "Except that I gather you have a family that's supportive."

There, she heard it again, that little ribbon of envy in his voice "And you had the Addams Family."

His smile faded into a grim line. "Yeah."

It was one thing to have differences, to disapprove of a family member's actions. It was another to turn your back on them in times of crisis. Try as she might, she couldn't wrap her mind around the latter. No matter what, they always came through for one another. She was living proof of that.

"And they really won't bail Eric out?"

He could feel his adrenaline rising again, his anger against his parents growing. They'd contributed to the man Eric was, or wasn't. They had no right to turn their backs on him like this.

"They'd be happy if Eric just conveniently faded away. Their only real concern is how this whole scandal reflects on them." He realized he'd begun pacing and forced himself to stop. "That's always been their only concern. The almighty reputation of the Garrisons." He shook his head. "With the kind of background Eric and I've had, it's a miracle we didn't turn out to be homicidal maniacs." The impact of his words hit him. He scrubbed his hand over his face. "Sorry, slip of the tongue."

A very bad slip, she thought. "I wouldn't do that

around people if I were you.'' She saw the suspicion
in his eyes as he looked at her. ''You don't have to
worry about me.''

No, he decided, he didn't. He glanced toward the
telephone and the menu he'd left beside it. He'd intended to order in after his shower. He still did. ''Are
you hungry? I can have something sent up.''

''I thought you already ate.''

''My lap had the Rigatoni Alfredo,'' he reminded
her. ''I didn't.''

She watched him reach for the phone. He was going
to call room service one way or another, and maybe
it wouldn't be too bad, having dinner with him in his
room. There was less noise to compete with.

Just as he raised the receiver to his ear, she said, ''I
put in for some personal time.''

''At the precinct?''

She nodded. He replaced the receiver into the cradle
again, puzzled.

''Why would you do that?'' he asked.

Because something was egging her on to give Eric's
case her full attention, despite the evidence against it.
''Because while I'm good at multitasking, I can't do
my job properly and look into your brother's case at
the same time. Too many feathers getting ruffled.''

By that he surmised she meant the police personnel.
He didn't want her doing anything that would place
her in harm's way. Or make valuable pieces of evidence disappear. ''Does anyone know you're looking
into it?''

''Longwell probably suspects something.'' She saw

his frown deepen and had to admit that it was a formidable sight. She wondered if he used it on the people who worked for him. "Don't worry about him, we go way back."

Cole was far from convinced that it was all right, but it wasn't that which prompted him to ask, "How far back?"

"We're friends, or were until I got my promotion."

"Jealousy?"

She doubted if Longwell had a jealous bone in his body, at least, not where work was concerned. He wasn't petty, like Patterson and some of the others, who had viewed her promotion as a form of nepotism.

"No, we just drifted apart. Different worlds," she explained. "There's a little bit of a caste system going on within the police department. We all band together when threatened from without, but internally—" she shrugged "— I guess it's no better or worse than every other place. One group doesn't quite trust the other."

He immediately thought of the investigation into Eric's case. "What did you mean by 'threatened from without'? You mean, when someone tries to shake a case?"

"Something like that." She nodded at the phone, making up her mind. She might as well stay. "You going to pick up that phone or does room service magically read your thoughts and deliver the meal of your choice at a set time?"

The sarcasm only made him laugh. It felt good, but it hardly went to relieve the tension pulsating within the room. "They might be able to read my thoughts, but not yours. I doubt if anyone can read yours."

Her smile was deceptively soft. "I'm a very simple person."

"I sincerely doubt that."

"I'll have whatever you're having," she informed him sweetly. "There, simple."

Not by a long shot, he thought.

The room had gotten somewhat warmer since she'd entered it. It seemed odd to him that in all the time he'd spent away from home, he'd never found himself more than passingly attracted to anyone. Throughout his travels, he'd had plenty of opportunities to find willing companionship. But beyond the physical, there'd never been any sort of real gratification. Which kept things simple but at the same time continued to propagate the feeling of isolation he carried around within him.

A hoped-for breakthrough in his brother's case seemed on the verge of happening.

Cole knew timing was everything, and whatever was in the making here couldn't have found the least opportune time to manifest itself. He had absolutely no time to think of himself right now. Because things were at a critical junction, he'd even gone so far as to delegate his work to his assistants so that he could be free for the length of time it took to prove Eric's innocence. But he had no time to pursue an urge that had materialized out of nowhere and might very well lead to the same place.

He picked up the telephone and ordered.

As she listened, Cole ordered Chicken Marsala, along with a bottle of wine, expensive by the sound of it.

"What," she asked as he hung up, amusement dancing along her lips, "no Alfredo sauce?"

She had a nice smile, he caught himself thinking. Not that it mattered one way or another.

"I've had enough of that to last me for a while," he said, turning away from the phone. "What does your gut instinct say?"

Her tongue threatened to seal itself up to the roof of her mouth again. *My gut instinct says I should get the hell out of here because the walls seemed to have moved in closer than they were a minute ago.*

"About what?" she asked.

"The report."

Idiot, she upbraided herself. Of course that's what he meant.

"Seems straightforward enough." She recited the highlights for him, although she had a feeling he was more familiar with them than she was. "Kathy Fallon was found dead in her apartment by a girlfriend who became worried that something might have happened to Kathy after she didn't come in to work and didn't answer her phone. She'd been stabbed." Rayne paused for a moment, then continued. "According to neighbors, Eric and Kathy were heard arguing rather heatedly that evening. He said something to the effect that if he couldn't have her, nobody could have her."

Cole took a deep breath. He was already aware of that and how damning this testimony was for Eric, but it was still circumstantial. "That doesn't automatically make him the killer. Eric said he left her alive."

"We can't find anyone to verify that," she told him quietly, "and Eric's fingerprints are all over the apartment. That, the restraining order Kathy swore out against him last month and the fact that he has no alibi for the time in question does put him at the head of the list."

"He was at the party," he reminded her.

She shook her head. She sympathized with what Cole seemed to be going through, because if it were one of her brothers facing being on trial for his life, she would be moving heaven and earth to try to find the flaw in the statement, the one piece that didn't fit or would give way. But right now, there didn't seem to be a tangible chink.

"Nobody remembers seeing Eric at the party after ten o'clock. The girl he was with supposedly said they were in one of the bedrooms and then she left. No one knows what happened to him after that. Kathy Fallon was killed close to midnight. By his own admission, Eric can't remember what happened to him between shortly after he got to the party and waking up to the sound of the police banging on his door." They might as well have everything out on the table at the same time. "And then there's the little matter of that imprint from Eric's ring on Kathy's face."

"I already told you, he said he gave it to her," Cole said.

"We just have his word for it."

He sighed, trying to gauge her tone. "So you think he did it?"

"No," she said honestly, "but the jury'll think he did it."

For the second time he stopped prowling around the room. He needed to know. "What makes you think he didn't?"

Cole's eyes seemed to pin her in place. Even though she felt for what he was going through, Rayne resented being probed this way. "Are you trying to mess with my head?"

He blew out a breath. He felt as if he had his back against a wall. All he could do was pray that it wasn't the wall in front of a firing squad.

"No, I'm trying to find what might be our best line of defense."

"I don't think Eric did it because the man I knew wouldn't have hurt anyone or anything. He didn't throw his weight around. He wanted everyone to like him. Dead people can't like you." She paused, knowing she hadn't really said anything they could use to sway a jury. "But I don't think using his character is going to be our best line of defense. Too many people out there have less than glowing things to say about Eric. In the last ten years he's gone from being a good-time Charlie to a rather pathetic little human being. He drank too much, spent too much and did nothing with his life except go from woman to woman. Until Kathy."

"Until Kathy," Cole echoed. There was a knock on the door. He saw the alert look instantly come over her face. In that moment he could almost visualize her springing into action. The notion tantalized him. He banked it down.

"Room service, remember?"

She was on edge. Whether it was due to the earlier call on her cell, or because she was here with Cole in what amounted to an intimate setting, she wasn't sure. All she knew was that a great deal of tension telegraphed itself up and down her body at an incredible rate.

She nodded toward the door. "Answer it."

As he went to open it, he noticed that Rayne slipped her hand inside her jacket. Was she reaching for her weapon for some reason? Just who did she expect to be coming to the door?

He had to admit that it was an odd feeling to have an armed woman in his room. He was no stranger when it came to guns. When he'd gone to South America posing as a mercenary with an intelligence cartel, he'd had to blast his way out of more than one situation. But the women he'd encountered during that brief period of his life had never handled any kind of weapon on a regular basis. This was a completely different experience for him.

But then, so was trying to get his brother absolved of a murder charge.

The person on the other side of the threshold when Cole opened the door was dressed in a short white jacket that contrasted with his neatly pressed black slacks. "Room service," the young man announced cheerfully.

Cole glanced over his shoulder at Rayne, his look all but saying, "See?"

"I'll take it from here," Cole told the waiter. He took possession of the cart after handing the young man a sizable tip.

Rayne closed the door the moment the cart was inside the room. "Well, you're certainly not stingy, I'll give you that," she murmured. He looked at her quizzically. "You gave that kid a twenty."

Since he'd begun working with people struggling to better themselves and the lives of their children, Cole had had a very profound sense of "there but for the grace of God...." It made him see things in a whole different light.

He positioned the table by the bed, then pulled over a chair for her. He figured she'd be more comfortable on it. Cole held it out, waiting for her. "Checking me out, Detective?"

Rayne sat down, letting him usher the chair in for her. "Just taking in bits and pieces of information. You never know when it might come in handy."

Cole reminded himself that she didn't need to be collecting information on him. And most of all, he didn't need to be so interested in her.

Cole took off the metal covers keeping the two dinners warm and slide them onto a shelf beneath the table. "I'm not the one facing trial."

"No, you're the black sheep who came back to save his brother."

How could you be a black sheep in a family that

was comprised of nothing *but* black sheep? He wondered if that was some kind of anomaly.

Cole sat down on the edge of the bed. "I'd prefer thinking of myself as a rebel."

"Sorry, that's my position. Or so they like to tell me."

By "they" he assumed she meant her family. Cole scoffed at the description. "You joined the police force like the rest of your family. How much of a rebel can you be?"

She felt as if he'd just challenged her. She still liked to think of herself in those terms, that she hadn't arrived at her present position in life without having gone through considerable angst. Angst that haunted her still at times. "And you made something of yourself rather than coast on your family's money. What kind of a black sheep are you?"

He broke open a roll. "I guess we're both reformed."

"In a manner of speaking." In her heart, she always knew she'd be a rebel. It had to do with a mind set. Determined to make her father proud of her and to make up for the years that had gone before, she still didn't intend to be mindlessly obedient to the department to which she'd pledged her loyalty.

"I still have my moments. Like now."

"Now?" The word shimmered between them invitingly. It made him think of warm moonlit nights and soft, supple bodies. Kisses that promised to go on forever, even when he knew they wouldn't.

Did her kisses do that?

Had she ever felt that strong pull that drew you into the eye of a hurricane before it spun you out to forever? Or had she been like him, seduced by the promise, only to be disappointed in the execution?

It took a moment before her words broke through. "I'm not exactly following official party line by independently looking into this for you, now am I?"

His smile, she found, was nothing short of raw sex. Her breath was coming in short supply. "Oh, that kind of now."

Finding her tongue was becoming an annoyingly repetitive task. "Yes, that kind of now."

She was doing more than justice to the dinner. He reached for the bottle chilling on the side. "Wine?"

Rayne placed her hand over the top of her glass before he had a chance to pour. "No."

Her response surprised him. He poured a little into his own glass. "Teetotaler?"

"Believe me, when I was younger, I drank enough alcohol to float a battleship." It wasn't something she was particularly proud of, but it was a fact and part of her past. She didn't see the point in trying to bury it by pretending she'd always been what she was today. Someone who, for the most part, walked a narrowed path. "But these days I like keeping a clear head." She looked at him significantly. "You never know when one might come in handy."

After taking a taste from his own glass, he retired it beside his plate. "Eric is going to need all the clear heads on his side he can get."

His gaze held her in place again. Dragging the breath out of her lungs. ''My thinking exactly.''

Suddenly he wasn't hungry anymore. Not for what room service had delivered. Not when there was this other thing buzzing around in his head, pushing other, more important thoughts out of the way. ''What else are you thinking?''

How did he do that? Evaporate the air around her? She was lucky she wasn't gasping. ''Nothing that has to do with Eric's case.''

''Yeah, me, too.'' He took a breath. There was no mistaking the look in her eyes. Not when it mirrored the one he was sure she saw in his. Slowly he rose to his feet, slipping his hand to her cheek. ''Want to get it out of the way?''

Rayne felt as if she were being levitated. She certainly wasn't gaining her feet under her own power. She didn't even try to pretend she didn't know what he was talking about. Because she did. ''Like a box we forgot to unpack?''

''Something like that.''

''You're on,'' she heard herself whispering.

And he was. The moment he kissed her, he was on. Completely turned on.

And unless he'd lost all ability to read another person, Cole knew for damn sure that he wasn't the only one.

Chapter 8

She wanted to get "it" out of the way. It. Her curiosity, about the kiss, about her response. About his. All tied up in one neat little bundle.

It.

She should have thought about getting herself out of the way. Wasn't that what you did when you were in the direct path of an oncoming steamroller? You jumped out of the way.

Except that she didn't.

And was completely and utterly flattened. Immediately.

It felt as if every available drop of air was pushed out of her lungs, her body. It left her head reeling and her pulse, she was fairly certain, had broken some kind of sound barrier limit because it throbbed so hard, so fast.

And the heat—there was a great deal of heat. Rayne would have sworn that she'd fallen headlong into hell, except that it felt like heaven.

Why else would there be music ringing in her head?

It wasn't music, it was bells. Bells were ringing. Even more appropriate. If such a word could be used to describe the scrambling sensations assaulting her body from every direction, making her acutely aware that she was a woman, a woman who had, of late, been living the life of a nun.

She didn't want to be a nun anymore.

It took Cole a second to realize that something *was* ringing. In the beginning, he'd felt sure the sound was only in his head, in his ears, reflecting the erratic way his heart was hammering.

Curiosity and a certain amount of overwhelming animal attraction had brought him to this junction. But what had begun as a minor thing now threatened to swallow him up whole. Because his curiosity wasn't sated, it was hungry for more.

He wanted her.

Of all the times...

With effort, Cole began to disengage himself from the tendrils wound tightly around him. He pulled his head away. The ringing left his ears and filled the room.

Idiot, he jeered silently to himself. "It's your phone," he finally told her.

"What?" The word escaped on the wave of a breathless gasp.

Were they still on earth? Still standing? Still in his room?

Could kisses *do* that? Completely obliterate your powers of orientation? She'd thought that was just a silly rumor, whispered amid pubescent girls nestled in sleeping bags at slumber parties while they still had their illusions and their dreams. Before reality found them.

Wonder filled her. Rayne felt like someone who had stumbled across the last living unicorn and was doubting her own eyes, her own senses.

"What?" she repeated, her breathing only a tad more controlled than before.

"Your phone." He nodded in the vague vicinity of her pocket. "It's ringing."

Rayne felt for her cell phone automatically, even as his words registered. Taking it out of her pocket, she opened the phone and she held it upside down to her ear. The smile on his lips made her realize her mistake.

She switched it right-side up with aplomb, daring him to laugh at her. Now if only she could unlock her knees without risking the embarrassment of sinking bonelessly to the floor.

The second she heard a noise on the other end, she straightened, remembering the last call. The whispered command.

"Hello?"

The voice on the other end of the line wasn't whispering. "Should I keep it warm for you?"

Heat still rushed to her face, her limbs. Bellhops carrying bags with no place to leave them. The last thing she needed was to keep anything warmer than it already was. "What?"

"Dinner," her father said patiently. "You want me to keep it warm for you? Or are you putting in extra time?"

You'd think that a former police chief wouldn't worry so much. But then, she amended, maybe he worried so much *because* he was a former police chief. Having him keep tabs on her used to annoy her no end, now she had to admit it just made her feel cared for. She wondered if she was getting wiser, or just older.

"Put dinner in the refrigerator," she said. *Put me in there with it while you're at it.*

She heard a long pause on the other end. "Rayne, are you all right? You sound different."

She still hadn't entirely caught her breath. She should have realized her father'd pick up on it. The man had ears that could put a bat to shame.

"Must be a bad connection, Dad. I'll see you later on tonight," she promised.

Rayne was vaguely aware of saying goodbye. Or maybe she just thought the words as she closed her phone and slipped it back into her pocket.

Cole watched her and she hadn't a clue what he was thinking. Had he been as blown out of the water as she was? Or was it just business as usual for him? At least he wasn't laughing at her.

Struggling for control, she blew out a long breath, then took another in. The light-headedness faded just a shade.

"Glad we got that out of the way," she murmured.

"I don't think we got anything out of the way," he told her. "But at least we answered one question."

She wasn't aware of anything being answered, only of a box being opened up and a thousand questions spilling out. Rayne blinked as her bangs fell into her eyes. "Oh?"

He resisted the urge to brush her hair aside, because then he'd be touching her and if he touched her, he might forget to stop. "It's not my imagination."

His eyes held hers, accelerating her pulse again. She pressed her lips together, tasting him. "Excuse me?"

"The tension that's been buzzing here between us. It's not just because I'm challenging police findings."

No, it wasn't, but she wasn't about to go exploring the issue any further until she had her bearings back. You didn't just waltz into a dark alley without knowing you could waltz back out again in one piece. It was one of the first lessons she'd learned not just at the academy, but at her father's knee.

She almost wished she was back there. Things had seemed so much more stable then. Her family had comprised her world and there were no dangers, no forbidding territories.

Rayne cleared her throat. "But that is the main reason we're here."

She shouldn't have had to remind him, Cole upbraided himself. Eric came first. If something was going to happen between him and Rayne, it would happen, but not now. Now it had to be put on ice.

Lots of ice.

"Right." Without thinking, Cole reached for his glass of wine. Then he stopped, changing his mind, and picked up the glass of water instead. Wine might just weaken his resistance enough to put himself first, Eric second. That was his parents' way, not his.

He drained the glass before he said anything. "While you were looking up the report today, I was going down the list."

She wasn't following him. "List, what list?"

"Of women Eric had gone out with in the last few years." He was as much trying to get some insight into the brother he'd left behind as he was trying to establish Eric's character. At some point in time, he knew he should have returned and taken Eric with him. Eric was weaker than he was, a good deal weaker, and had wound up selling his soul because it was easier that way than it was to attempt to make something of himself. Cole frowned. "Some of the things they had to say about him weren't all that flattering."

Putting some distance between them, Rayne moved over to the window. It began to mist outside. "And you're thinking of using them as character witnesses?"

He heard the incredulous note in her voice. "The point is, none of them said Eric ever raised a hand to them, ever threatened them, ever turned remotely ugly. At best, he was a sloppy drunk, harmless. One of them even called him giddy."

She knew what he was trying to do, but that approach would get them nowhere. She remembered what Longwell had said to her. That everyone was capable of murder under the right circumstances. "The D.A.'ll say that everyone's got their breaking point. And there are those neighbors who'll testify that they overheard Kathy and Eric in a shouting match, arguing."

He shook his head. "Eric doesn't argue or shout. He withdraws. He cries."

"But Kathy was different," she reminded him. "She meant something to him."

He was pacing again, his agitation clearly rising as he absently ran his hand through his hair. Watching him, Rayne caught herself wondering what that same hand would feel like running along her body. Caressing her. Finding all the secret places.

She stopped herself abruptly.

What was she, seventeen? She was twenty-five, for heaven's sake, and far from a trembling, inexperienced teenager. Hell, she hadn't been all that inexperienced as a teenager, either.

Then what was going on? Why was she having all this trouble focusing on what mattered? Maybe she was coming down with something. It seemed to be the only explanation, at least, the only explanation she'd accept.

Cole suddenly swung around to face her, excitement in his eyes as he worked out a theory. "These neighbors that supposedly overheard Kathy and Eric arguing, did they actually *see* them arguing?"

She thought of the report she'd reread after she'd talked to Longwell.

"Maybe." He continued looking at her, as if he expected her to amend her answer. She did. "There wasn't any mention of anyone actually seeing anything. But there were several statements in agreement—" The excitement had increased. She could feel herself being reeled in. "What are you getting at?"

He had to admit it was a long shot, but it was possible. More than possible, it struck him as perhaps the only explanation. "What if she wasn't arguing with Eric? What if everyone just assumed it was Eric because she had that restraining order out on him? What if," he hypothesized, "it was someone else?"

"And that someone else killed her?" she guessed. When he nodded, she shook her head. He'd already said something like that before, when he thought Eric was being framed. It was wishful thinking on his part. "You're reaching for straws, Garrison."

He didn't waver. "That doesn't mean there aren't any there."

Stranger things had turned out to be right, who was she to ignore a possibility? "Okay, I can check that out tomorrow."

"We," he corrected. "We can check it out tomorrow."

She was trying to attract the least amount of attention. Having him with her wasn't going to accomplish that. Cole Garrison was as unmemorable as a meteor shower. "Look, let's not get in each other's way."

"Fine. I'll stand two steps to your right at all times."

"Cole—"

He purposely kept his expression innocent. "Would you prefer the left?"

She would prefer it if he were out of the picture entirely. "Cole, do you know one of the reasons the South lost the war?" He looked stunned by the question. Just as she'd wanted him to be. "Too many leaders, not enough soldiers."

"In the middle of all this, you're stopping to give me a history lesson?" he asked incredulously. "For somebody who supposedly never studied in high school, you're just chock-full of information, aren't you?"

She'd lost track of the number of times the principal had sent for her father because she wasn't doing her homework or was cutting classes. The thing Principal Oshinsky could never understand was how she managed to do so well on tests when she'd hardly even put in a regular appearance in class. Back then, she couldn't abide structure or any rules that hemmed her in. That didn't mean she was stupid.

Rayne shrugged. "I liked doing independent studies."

"Maybe that's our problem. We're both too independent."

"Agreed. The bottom line is, I can't have you compromising the investigation."

He wasn't about to sit in the hotel, cooling his heels while she did the legwork. He wanted to be right there with her. "I'd say we were compromising it just by being in the mix."

She hated to admit it, but he was right. Having her

look into the case could already be considered a compromising circumstance if it came to light. She had to
be very careful how she went about things. Enemies
in the department didn't go away easily.

One look at Cole told her that he wasn't about to
be kept out of it. Like he said, they were kindred spirits of a sort and if this had been about one of her own,
someone would have had to tie her down. "All right,
but we still have to do it my way."

Cole spread his hands out to either side of him, as
if in complete compliance with her terms. "As long
as I get to be there."

She knew she would never convince him otherwise.
It was better to have him beside her than to have to
keep looking over her shoulder to see where he was.
Though he struck her as pretty savvy, she couldn't
take a chance on his jeopardizing the investigation by
tainting their findings.

She crossed to the door. It was time to go before
she decided to revisit the site of her encounter with
the steamroller. "Okay, I'll stop by at nine and pick
you up tomorrow morning."

His expression was unfathomable and made her a
little uneasy as he nodded. Cole reached around her to
open the door for her. "It's a deal."

She noticed that he hadn't bothered to shake on it.

Rayne glanced at her watch. She was running late
again. Stifling an oath, she strapped on her gun, then
slipped her jacket on over it.

Andrew eased a frying pan into sudsy water. Rayne was the last one in the kitchen. "I thought you said you weren't going in today."

"I'm not. That doesn't mean I'm not going to go out."

"What's up, kiddo? Tell your old man."

She didn't want to tell him because she didn't want a lecture. She picked up her coat. The weatherman promised more rain was on the way. It never ceased to amaze her how her siblings could get away without a third degree, but she'd always had to jump through hoops when it came to their father.

Probably because she'd given him so much to worry about when she was younger. None of her brothers or sisters had ever had to have him come down to the police station to fetch them. In hindsight, it had been a harmless prank, but the Aurora police department hadn't thought so at the time.

"Nothing's up, Dad. I'm just running a few errands, catching up on things. Doing a favor for a friend."

The frying pan sank below the suds, sending foam over the side. He ignored it. His attention was on his daughter's last words. And her manner. "What kind of a favor?"

She was already out of the kitchen, heading for the front door and freedom. "The kind that needs doing."

"Rayne—"

"Probably," she called over her shoulder. "I'll be sure to take an umbrella."

Throwing open the door, she managed to make good her escape.

And come very close to slamming into Cole.

Swallowing a gasp of surprise, she took half a step back. With the door at her back, there was no place for her to go.

Instantly her temper flared. Was he spying on her? "I thought we had a deal."

Amusement tugged on his lips. She looked breathless, as if she'd made a run for the door. Breathless looked good on her. He didn't allow his thoughts to go any further than that.

"The thing about deals is that when they involve more than one person, as they perforce need to, they have a tendency to fluctuate." Before she could say anything, he indicated his car parked across the street. He'd positioned it to look as if he was visiting the people on the other end of the block. "I did sit in the car and wait for everyone else to leave," he pointed out. Which brought him to a question of his own. He'd counted more than half a dozen cars coming and going since he'd arrived. "Just how many people stop by here in the morning, anyway? I've seen less traffic at roadside diners during rush hour."

He watched a hint of a smile curve her lips. "My father likes to feed the family."

He came from an almost nonexistent family. His mother was an only child and his father had one brother whom he despised. Cole'd heard the feeling was mutual. The concept of a large family never quite registered, certainly not one that had enough members to make up a small country of its own.

"All those people were related to you?"

She nodded. "In one fashion or another. Siblings, cousins, about-to-be spouses to siblings."

That took care of the adults. But there'd been more. "And the two kids?"

He meant Brent's daughter and Clay's newly discovered son. Something she didn't feel she had the right to get into without Clay's okay. "Long story."

"Which you're not going to tell me."

Not wanting her father to see her talking to Cole, she began to urge him off the property. "Maybe some other time."

Too late. Her escape was terminated. The door behind them opened and Andrew was in the doorway, giving Cole the once-over. Slowly.

Rayne held her breath. Waiting for an explosion of some sort to erupt.

"You must be Garrison."

To her knowledge, her father had never met the man, now or when he was in high school. She blew out a breath. "How do you do that?"

Gray-blue eyes twinkled at her. "Trade secret. Keeps me one step ahead of my kids. A place where all parents want to be." His eyes shifted back toward Cole, taking measure. Closely. He put his hand out. "Andrew Cavanaugh."

"Pleased to meet you."

"We'll see," Andrew replied, dropping his hand to his side again. "Sorry to hear about your brother."

Here it comes, Cole thought, bracing himself for a confrontation. Authority figures still had that kind of effect on him. And he on them. After all, this was Aurora, the place where he'd been the outsider. "He's innocent."

If Andrew heard the edge in Cole's voice, he gave no indication. His expression remained unchanged. Instead he spared a glance at his daughter.

"So Rayne seems to think. You have anything to go on besides gut feelings?" He addressed the question to Cole.

"We're working on it."

Andrew nodded. Then, instead of a lecture, or the promise of one, he completely surprised Rayne by saying to Cole, "Let me know if there's anything I can do."

With that, he withdrew, leaving Rayne standing on the doorstep with a stunned expression on her face.

Cole peered at her as the door closed behind them. "You okay?"

She shook her head, as if to free her brain of cobwebs. "Who was that masked man?" she murmured.

"What?"

Rayne waved her hand. "Nothing. It's just that I would have expected him to say something about the possible fallout over what we're doing."

"Because he's a straight arrow?"

She glanced over her shoulder, not completely certain that her father still might not come out.

"Because he doesn't want me stirring up any trouble for myself." She started to put on her coat. Cole took it from her, holding it so that she could slip her arms into the sleeves. She offered him an absent smile in response. "He tends to be very protective that way."

"Maybe he thinks the truth is worth a little trouble."

"Maybe," she agreed.

She glanced over her shoulder one last time at the closed door. It just went to show her that just when she thought she had her father all figured out, he pulled something like this on her.

With a confused shrug, she headed toward her car. Cole took her arm. "You're putting yourself out for me. The least I can do is drive."

She didn't want it on that footing. Didn't want this getting any more personal than it had already gotten. Deep down, where it counted, personal had always scared the hell out of her.

"I'm not putting myself out for you," she informed him, summoning her best professional, distant manner. However, she did take him up on his offer and walked over to his car. After all, it *was* a Porsche. "I'm doing it so that I can feel the right man is being charged with the crime."

Experience had taught him not to look a gift horse in the mouth. What mattered was that it was there, that she was helping. Everything else, he had to remember, was secondary.

"Whatever works for you," he said, opening the passenger side for her.

Right now, very little was working, Rayne thought as she slid into the seat. She glanced at Cole as he rounded the hood and got into the car beside her.

Least of all her willpower.

Chapter 9

Rayne could feel frustration building up inside of her. She didn't like going around in circles and that was exactly what they'd been doing since they'd arrived at Sunflower Apartments. Taking down statements and going nowhere.

As they left the apartment of a very talkative woman who'd jumped at the chance to have some live company instead of her daily dose of talk show hosts, Rayne glanced in Cole's direction.

His face betrayed nothing but she could sense the tension inside. They needed a break in the case and they needed it soon.

They'd spent the better part of the day canvassing the area around Kathy Fallon's garden apartment, talking not just to the neighbors who resided in close proximity, but to anyone who might have had an occasion to pass her apartment. The front faced one of the larger parking areas. Someone had to have heard or seen something useful. But finding that "someone" meant going door to door and talking to a great many of the people living within the two hundred and fifteen units that comprised the complex. Because it was a Tuesday and the middle of the day, not everyone was in.

Rayne kept track of the apartments where someone *was* in, making notes to which units had not opened their doors to them. By four, they'd made a good-size dent—and still gotten nowhere. No new piece of information surfaced to substantiate Cole's idea that Kathy had been arguing with someone else the day she'd been killed.

No one responded in the apartment of the man who lived directly above Kathy. They returned three times to check. Each time the knock went unanswered. They needed a lead. Unrealistically, Rayne began pinning her hopes on him. She found herself as caught up in the case as Cole was.

Coming down the stairs after another futile attempt, Rayne stopped in front of Kathy's apartment. Yellow tape still demarcated the area as a crime scene. She looked at the door for a long moment, fighting with her conscience. Her conscience lost.

"Come on," she finally announced just as Cole had begun to walk to another group of apartments. Of the six apartments clustered there, they'd only found someone home in two of them so far.

He turned around and crossed back to her. "We're leaving?"

Rayne took a deep breath. "No, technically, we're violating a crime scene." Reaching into the pockets of her coat, she took a pair of thin plastic gloves out of each of them. She held one set out to Cole.

Taking them, he looked at her. "How many pairs do you have there?"

"Just two." She began slipping her pair on. "I like being prepared."

And these days, she was, for anything that might come her way. *Except,* the voice in her head taunted, *for a man who looks like the personification of sin.*

Rayne cleared her throat, as if that could somehow clear the thought from her brain, as well. "Sometimes one pair has a hole in it."

Cole glanced down at the pair he was pulling on. "Mine looks okay."

"Good to know," she murmured.

Cole had his doubts about this. Though he wanted to prove Eric's innocence at all costs, he thought of the ramifications of illegally entering a crime scene area. This wasn't some TV crime show where anything went down. This was real. Everything had to be done by the book to stand up in court where documentation was paramount.

He stopped Rayne before she could move the yellow tape. "Won't we be disturbing things?"

The crime scene was two weeks old and the tape scheduled to come down soon. Only a shortage of manpower had prevented it from happening already. "The detectives and forensics went over this place with a fine-tooth comb. Everything that needs to be recorded has already been photographed to death.''

He nodded toward the tape stretched out over the door and the banner that was strung up from one wall to the other in front of it, forming a tiny alcove of its own. ''Then why's the tape still up?''

''They haven't gotten around to taking it down,'' she assured him.

He looked around to see if anyone was watching. ''Is there any point to us going in?''

''Two more sets of eyes. Fresh perspective,'' she enumerated. She looked at him. ''You might see something that everyone else missed.'' At least, that was what she was hoping.

Unlike Rayne, he doubted they would find anything new. He didn't know Eric anymore, not in the day-to-day, mundane sense of the word. Didn't know his likes, his dislikes or what he did with himself when he wasn't sitting in a jail cell.

What he did know was the essence of the man. Knew beyond reason that his brother couldn't kill anyone. But as for being able to spot some kind of glaring inconsistency, Cole sincerely doubted that was going to happen.

But he said nothing, trusting in what he hoped were Rayne's keen instincts. That and witnesses who hadn't turned up yet was all he had to base his hope on.

Cole followed her lead, ducking under the first length of yellow tape. As he watched, she carefully broke the seal on the door. There was no way she could reseal it without showing signs of entry.

"Won't they notice?"

She come prepared for that, too. Digging into her purse, Rayne held up a small roll of yellow tape she'd brought along.

"No," she replied simply.

Cole shook his head. There was a great deal more to the woman than he'd thought at first. He thought of the reputation she'd had in high school. Back then, no one would have put anything past her. She lived her entire life on a dare.

"There's still larceny in your soul, isn't there?"

"Only the good kind."

The door was locked, but she got around that, too. It wasn't a difficult lock to pick. Easing open the door, she took two steps into the single-bedroom residence and came to an abrupt halt.

There were dried pools of blood on the beige carpet. A harsh chalk outline was all that was left to remind her that a flesh-and-blood person had died there.

Cole looked over her shoulder. "It's not going to be easy renting out this place."

That was where he was wrong. "A little sanitizing, a new carpet, you'd be surprised." She got her wind back. Death always took it away from her. Maybe because it always made her think of her mother. "Some people," she went on, "actually like living in a place where a murder was committed." Turning around, she looked at him. "Makes them feel as if they're living on the edge."

He just shook his head. "Crazy world."

"Amen to that." Rayne scanned the area quickly.

There was no sign of a struggle. If Kathy Fallon had offered resistance, it was minimal. "It was an easy kill. He caught her off guard." Her eyes came back to rest on Cole's face. "Like she felt that the person she was talking to couldn't hurt her."

"Most people feel that way unless the person they're with had displayed violent tendencies before." His mouth curved in an ironic smile. He was thinking of his own days in Bogota. "We're all pretty much secure in our immortality."

She wondered if he spoke from experience, or if it was just a philosophy he was tossing around. In either case, it made sense. But, "Maybe," was all she allowed.

Methodically, Rayne began going through drawers, shelves, bedding, looking for anything that might give them a clue to the man—or woman—who had done this. She noted that Cole followed suit.

"Make sure you leave everything the way you found it."

"This isn't my first time."

Her fingers froze for a moment. "You've gone through dead people's apartments before?"

"Let's just leave it at what I've said."

He was stirring up questions in her head again, questions about who and what he was beyond the drop-dead gorgeous man in the next room. It occurred to her that she only had his word for his past. Maybe she should have done more than researched his present way of life, maybe she should have gone back over the past ten years before she'd allowed herself to feel comfortable around him.

Who was she kidding? She wasn't comfortable around him. She felt as if she was just stepping onto a tightrope stretched out over Niagara Falls. One misstep and she would plummet.

The search, like their canvassing, turned up nothing. At least, nothing in their favor. There was a host of love letters from Eric that Kathy kept in a folder. If you despised the man or were afraid of him, why keep his letters? There was nothing damning in them. They were the sophomoric ramblings of a man in love. A man in love who had no love for grammar.

After reading through several, she stopped and shook her head. "How did they ever let your brother graduate high school? I don't know which was worse, his grammar or his spelling."

"Neither was a capital offense the last time I checked."

His voice was weary, Rayne thought. He obviously felt as discouraged as she did. "Well, at least we know she knew her assailant," Rayne concluded as she walked out of the bedroom. The room was beyond neat. The whole apartment was. She didn't trust anyone who was so neat. It spoke of someone who was too controlling. Her own room looked as if it was home to several typhoons. "There's no sign of forced entry, no breaking and entering."

"Unlike you."

Startled, she swung around to see that Longwell was

Dangerous Games

standing in the doorway, his wide features creased with a disapproving frown.

"What are you doing here, Rayne?" he asked. Longwell fixed accusing brown eyes on the man standing next to her. "With *him*?" It was hard to miss the contempt in his voice.

Cole saw her lift her chin, pulling her shoulders back just a shade. Becoming defensive. For some reason she made him think of the statue of Justice he'd seen outside the courthouse. The word "magnificent" whispered along his brain.

"We're just looking around," she told the other policeman.

Longwell's frowned deepened. He completely ignored Cole's presence. "You're violating protocol, you know that? It's not your case."

Rayne fell back on a friendship that was once far stronger than it was now. "Oh, c'mon, Longwell, we're not disturbing anything." She saw the look entering the man's eyes as they passed over the area. Things began to fall into place. Because they'd once been close, she wouldn't allow herself to take umbrage at the implication. "We're certainly not going to plant anything. I just thought a fresh perspective—"

He cut her off. "You're not supposed to think, not about this case." Longwell waved her off. "Go think about your own cases. Just because you made detective faster than anyone in the department doesn't give you the right to break rules—no matter what kind of bloodlines you have."

Her eyes narrowed. "What are *you* doing here, if

you don't mind my asking?'' He'd popped up far too conveniently for her liking.

''The woman in 115 called me.'' He nodded vaguely off in the direction of the apartment in question. ''Said that there were two police detectives going around, asking questions.'' His accusing look rested only briefly on Cole, dismissing him as money and no brains. ''She'd already given her statement to me, and then to Rollins and Webber and she thought it a little odd that she was being asked again, so she called me. I'd left my card with her in case she remembered something,'' he added.

Just her luck, Rayne thought. ''Very efficient of you.''

Longwell laughed shortly. His lips didn't curve. ''You're not the only one who wants to move up in the ranks.''

Since when had Longwell exhibited any signs of ambition? At the academy he'd preferred coasting to studying. Though bright, he did just enough work to pass and graduate. ''I'm not trying to move up, I'm just trying to help a friend.''

''So, he's a friend now, is he?'' As if aware that he'd crossed over a line, Longwell sighed and relented. ''You find anything?''

She frowned. ''No, we didn't.''

Longwell indicated the front door. ''Then you two had better get out of here before I have to report this.''

His cooperation surprised her. This was more like the Longwell she'd once known. ''Then you won't?''

"No." He put a condition on it. "Not if the two of you leave now."

There was no point to remaining in the apartment, although she wanted to continue canvassing the area. But that was something they were going to have to do when Longwell wasn't around. For now she nodded. "Fair enough."

Longwell waited until she and Cole were both out before he followed in their wake. Pulling the door shut, he paused to look at the cut yellow barricade.

"I'm going to have to get some new tape—" He stopped as Rayne held up the roll she'd brought with her. "You turn into a Girl Scout?"

She grinned. "Something like that."

Giving the roll to Longwell, she looked at Cole. The latter nodded his agreement. They'd been at it for close to eight hours, stopping only to grab something to eat at a drive-thru located in the shopping center a mile away. Maybe it *was* time to call it a day.

Taking her arm, Cole ushered her over to his car. Being around Longwell and the man's smug attitude got under his skin. He was afraid he'd be tempted to say something.

"I'll drop you off at your house," Cole told her as he opened the door on his side. He could see Longwell watching them.

Rayne thought they should come back tomorrow to finish talking to the neighbors. One of them had seen something, even if they didn't know they had. She was beginning to like Cole's theory about there being someone else, even though some of the neighbors said that they'd never seen another man entering Kathy's apartment, other than Eric and the police officer who'd taken Kathy's statement.

Rayne replayed Cole's words. He'd left something unsaid. "Where will you go?"

"To see Eric."

"To question him some more?"

"To comfort him," he contradicted. He felt sorry for his brother, now more than ever. From everything he'd seen in the apartment, Kathy Fallon had come across as a cold, controlling woman. Eric needed warmth. "He's got to be down—and scared. I know neither one of my parents has been by and I doubt if any of the people he hung out with have bothered to pay him a visit." They hadn't as of the last time he'd spoken to his brother. "Eric didn't exactly associate with people who knew the meaning of the word friendship."

She felt too wired to go home yet. "If you're going to the station, I'll come with you."

She saw a wariness enter his eyes. To some degree, she supposed they were still waltzing around distrust. Nobody had ever done anything for Cole without a reason. That went a long way to creating a suspicious adult. She counted herself lucky to have had the up-bringing, the home life that she'd had, even though she hadn't always been smart enough to appreciate it.

"There's a couple of things I want to check out. I'll probably still be at it by the time you leave." She knew he wouldn't welcome sitting around, cooling his heels. "Don't worry, you don't have to hang around. I can get someone to drop me off."

He wanted to say that hanging around waiting for her was no hardship, but that would have been revealing too much. And putting himself in a position he had no intentions of occupying.

So he merely nodded and turned the car toward the police station.

The visit with Eric left him more determined than ever to get his brother out of jail. Eric was becoming a nervous wreck, constantly fidgeting, hardly able to sit still for more than a few minutes at a time. Eric wasn't going to be able to take much more of this. Certainly not an extended period behind bars.

He had to get Eric free.

If this had been a jail cell in Bogota, Cole knew what he would have done. He would have brushed a few palms with the right amount of money, gotten his hands on the fastest vehicle he could and broken Eric out.

But that kind of life was behind him now by more than a couple of years. He much preferred where he was to where he'd been, even though freedom carried rules with it that shackled a person at times.

There had to be a way around that.

Everything he'd learned today from the neighbors confirmed that Eric had been in love with Kathy Fallon, in love probably for the first time in his life, just as he'd said. And the feeling hadn't been returned. One woman told them that, just before Kathy had taken out the restraining order, Eric had actually hired a band to serenade her. Kathy had loudly belittled him and sent the musicians away.

Cole shook his head as he got into his car. Kathy had probably reminded Eric of their mother. Certainly the framed photograph he'd seen on the coffee table in the dead woman's apartment had sent an eerie chill down his back. There was more than a passing resemblance between Kathy Fallon and the way his mother had looked some twenty years ago.

Poor Eric, he thought as he pulled out of the police station parking lot. Even when he'd finally fallen in love with someone, it was the wrong kind of woman.

At least his brother was drawn to someone. Cole had never felt that magic surge through him that Eric had sadly described tonight. That sense of blessed wonder that filled his soul whenever he was around her.

Hell, the closest he had come to that kind of thing was—

Abruptly, Cole stopped himself.

He wasn't going to go there. It was just his frustration talking.

And maybe, just maybe, his loneliness.

With the news of the past few days, he'd left chinks of himself open. Chinks that had allowed emotions to slip in and to color his views.

A temporary aberration and nothing more, he silently insisted.

He was fine just the way he was, moving from place

to place, doing some good whenever he could. He didn't need anything different in his life.

Certainly not any*one* different in his life.

The rain that had been flirting with the air all day finally decided to fall. A fine mist covered his windshield. Flipping on his wipers, Cole turned his vehicle down the winding road, which eventually led to his hotel.

A car suddenly pulled out just in front of him before darting into the next lane, its turn signal flashing belatedly.

Biting off a curse, Cole slammed on his brakes a moment before the offending vehicle switched lanes. His car didn't slow down. Didn't respond at all.

A sense of alarm infiltrated his being.

He tried the brakes again.

Nothing happened.

The car began to pick up speed.

There was no reason for the failure. His brakes weren't wet. It had only been raining for a few minutes and there'd been no deep puddles for him to have traveled through, incapacitating the brakes. What the hell was going on?

Trees on either side of the road shook their heads in the rising wind like darkly cloaked prophets of doom. Cole tried the brakes again, tapping them in sharp, quick succession.

The brakes didn't respond. The incline was becoming more pronounced.

Cole looked around for somewhere he could safely stop the car. The traffic was light, but at any second that could change. He couldn't take a chance on crashing into another car.

Steering as best he could, he spotted a tree up ahead and aimed for that, reasoning that his air bag would take the brunt of the impact.

Suddenly, Cole saw a boy walking his dog. The boy wore a dark, hooded jacket and hadn't been visible until just now. Swearing, sweating, Cole twisted the steering wheel to the opposite side, avoiding the collision at the last moment.

Gaining speed.

The boy jump out of the way, yanking his dog with him. Somewhere in the background, Cole thought he heard a woman scream, but he couldn't be sure. His entire attention was focused on trying to find someplace he could use to stop his vehicle. He prayed that the air bag would deploy.

The road directly ahead of him curved sharply. A row of condominiums, close to the street, was on his left, a well-manicured play area hugging the curve was on the right. The play area was empty.

Any second now he was going to crash into one of the houses.

Digging up prayers he could hardly remember from his childhood, windshield wipers slapping time, Cole steered his car toward the play area as best he could.

Tires hit the curb, flying over it, smashing into the fire hydrant and sending a geyser into the air.

The car finally stopped.

The air bag didn't deploy.

Chapter 10

"Ohmigod, are you all right?"

Bursting out of Shaw's car the moment her brother brought it up behind the totaled Porsche, Rayne rushed to Cole's side. He was leaning against what was left of his red vehicle, holding a bloodstained handkerchief against his forehead. The gash he'd received when his head met the steering wheel was still bleeding. He looked unsteady to her.

He'd called her less than fifteen minutes ago, his voice sounding strained. Strange. The second he'd said he'd been in an accident, she'd fired a single question at him. Where was he? He'd only been able to give her a vague description.

Ordering him to stay put, she'd called Shaw and told him to meet her at the front door. He was the only one of her siblings still at the police station. She'd seen

him at his desk earlier, putting in overtime to finish
reports that had been due at the end of the last month.
It was one of the things they all had in common. They
put off filling out reports until the last possible moment.

Not waiting for Cole to speak, she answered her
own rhetorical question. "Of course you're not all
right. Here, sit," she ordered, guiding him to the seat
behind the driver's in Shaw's car. Once she had him
down, she held up her hand, wiggling several digits.
"How many fingers am I holding up?"

"All of them." It felt as if someone was using a
sledgehammer to reconstruct his skull from the inside
out. With effort, he waved her hand away. "I'm all
right. I just need a minute, that's all." He looked at
the condition of the car he'd crawled out of once he'd
come to. The nose could have doubled as an accor-
dion. It took very little imagination to realize that he'd
come very close to being killed. "And a way to get
to the hotel."

"You're not going to the hotel, you're going to the
hospital," she informed him in no uncertain terms.

With a sigh, Cole looked past her at the man who
was taking close scrutiny of the wreckage whose nose
was halfway up the lamppost. "Is there any way you
could drop me off?"

"Tell him he has to go to the hospital," Rayne in-
structed her brother.

Temporarily abandoning his perusal of the wrecked
vehicle, Shaw crossed back to Cole and gave the
man's wound and his overall state a once-over.

"You could use a stitch or two, but a tightly applied butterfly bandage'll do almost the same job."

"Shaw!" Rayne cried sharply.

He shrugged. "Sorry, kid, I call them the way I see them."

Cole nodded, or tried to. The interior reconstruction of his head was now being accompanied by the "Overture of 1812," complete with cannon. "Good."

She didn't think it was good at all. What was it with men? What was this macho thing they felt they had to invoke?

"You'll scar," she pointed out.

His mouth curved in a semismile. "Won't be the first time. Besides, I hear scars are supposed to be sexy," Cole muttered.

She'd grown up with countless men in her life and knew when it was pointless to argue. Rayne turned her attention to another question. "What happened? Did you swerve to avoid something?" Although he should have seen it, she thought. This particular area was better lit than the rest of the winding road.

Cole struggled to pull his mind into focus. "A kid and his dog, but that wasn't the problem."

The words were coming more easily now, and the fog was finally beginning to lift from his brain. When he'd first come to, he'd suffered more than a few minutes of complete confusion. Events from his life had all glued themselves together in his head. Past, present, they'd all come together like one giant jumble that initially defied untangling.

He remembered the onset of panic. "The brakes

didn't work.'' The final moment of impact replayed itself in his aching mind. "Neither did the air bag.''

Shaw was already looking beneath the hood, around the engine. He aimed his flashlight toward where the front and back brake lines ran. "That's because the brakes have been cut.''

Rayne turned sharply. "Cut?'' She hurried over to see for herself. Shaw shone his flashlight over the tell-tale area. "We drove to Kathy's Fallon's apartment complex and back in that car.'' She thought of the sudden stop Cole'd had to come to just before the police station when a car had pulled out in front of them. "The brakes worked fine then.''

"They're not working fine anymore,'' Shaw said simply. Moving around Rayne, Shaw shone his flash-light inside the crumpled vehicle. From all appear-ances, the air bag was still inside its case. "Neither was the air bag.'' He looked at Cole. "The mechanism to deploy the air bag has been tampered with.''

An icy feeling passed over her. Rayne exchanged looks with Cole. She didn't like what she was hearing. Someone had deliberately tried to kill him.

"It had to have happened while you were inside the station, visiting Eric.''

"That'd be my guess,'' Shaw agreed. Flipping off the flashlight, he tossed it back into his car's glove compartment. His easygoing manner vanished as fury entered his eyes. "You could have just as easily been in the car with him.'' He didn't bother looking in Cole's direction, his attention completely focused on his sister. "Somebody doesn't want you investigating this. Damn it, Rayne, what the hell have you got your-self involved in this time?''

Her brother was right in everything he was thinking. It didn't take a genius to figure it out. He didn't have any right to put her in harm's way like this, Cole thought. ''I want you to back off,'' Cole told her. ''I'll take it from here.''

Back off.

Those were the exact words used to threaten her on her cell. She didn't take orders very well, never had. That they were now coming from her brother and Cole only served to infuriate her.

Rayne fisted her hands on her waist. Who the hell did they think they were, deciding what she was going to do or not going to do?

''If you need someone on the inside,'' Shaw was saying to Cole, ''I'll handle it.''

Okay, this had gone far enough. She was a police detective, damn it, not some porcelain doll to be placed in the china closet.

Rayne placed herself between the two men. ''Just a damn minute here. Before the two of you form some good ol' boys club and start making up the charter, there's something you should know. I am not about to be scared off, threatened off, or told by my big brother to bug off, understand?'' She looked from one to the other. ''I'm a big girl, I can wipe my own nose and handle my own cases. Got that?''

''This isn't your case,'' Shaw pointed out.

''It is now—'' Her voice faltered only slightly as she added, ''unofficially.'' She knew there was no way she could go to her superior and ask to be assigned to it. Her personal involvement at this point disqualified her. ''I am not about to drop out and let you take over,'' she told Shaw. ''This isn't up for discussion.'' That said, she gave getting Cole medical attention one more try. ''C'mon, Shaw, we need to take him to the hospital—''

''Hotel,'' Cole said just as adamantly. He wasn't about to sit in some ER, cooling his heels for half the night, waiting for treatment of something that was far from fatal. ''That's not up for discussion, either. I've suffered a hell of a lot worse.''

Her eyes narrowed. She didn't believe him. ''When?'' she challenged.

''That's not up for discussion, either,'' he repeated. Since he was already partially in the car, Cole shifted in the seat, pulling in his legs. Very carefully, he reached for the door and shut it. His message was clear. He was terminating the conversation.

With a huff, Rayne got into the passenger side beside her brother.

''Take him to the hotel,'' she said.

She missed the knowing look that had slipped over Shaw's face.

They pulled up a little shy of the hotel's main entrance, bypassing a squadron of eager valets. Cutting off the engine, Shaw got out on his side, then offered his arm to Cole. Ignoring it, Cole struggled out of the car on his own power.

''Thanks for the ride.''

Cole's words seemed to be addressed to both of them. There was no way she was letting him go up to his room alone. His wound needed tending.

As he began to walk away, Rayne called after him, "Wait for me at the door." And then she looked at her brother. "Why don't you go home? I'll catch a cab later."

But Shaw shook his head. "I'll leave you my car. I can catch a cab."

That meant she'd have to go to his place and then have him drive her over to hers. There were too many logistics involved. "But—"

Shaw considered himself relatively easygoing, but every once in a while, she managed to push him over the edge. Like now. Why couldn't she be like Patrick's sister? Patience was a vet. You could go an entire lifetime without worrying about someone pumping a bullet into a vet.

"Damn it, Rayne, for once in your life, just stop arguing."

"I will if you will," she retorted. "Takes two to make an argument, you know."

Shaw blew out a breath. "I've just got one question."

Rayne glanced over her shoulder toward the entrance. Cole was waiting. He hadn't made a break for it. That was a hopeful sign.

"What?" she asked impatiently.

"How long have you had a thing for Cole Garrison?"

Her head whipped back around. Coming out of nowhere, Shaw's question had caught her completely off balance. She let indignation color her cheeks. "I don't have a 'thing' for Cole Garrison."

But Shaw merely smiled. "Looked in any good mirrors lately?" She raised her brow quizzically. This time, he grinned. "It's written all over your face."

"Shut up and go home, Shaw." With that, she shoved the keys at him and hurried over to Cole. After a moment she heard him start up the car.

It felt good to win an argument once in a while, she thought as she took her place beside Cole.

He indicated the departing vehicle, taking care not to move his head too abruptly. "What was that all about?"

There was no way she was going to give Cole a complete narrative, especially not since he'd been the centerpiece of it. "Just a little territorial struggle over who got the car and who called a cab."

He saw Shaw turn left onto the busy street that ran past the precinct. He hadn't thought the man the type to strand his sister. "You lost?"

Whatever gave him that idea? "I won."

Maybe it was the head injury, but he wasn't following her. "But your brother just took the car."

Because he still looked a little unsteady to her, she skipped going through the revolving doors and opened one of the side doors instead. After a beat, he walked through it first. "I know."

The quizzical look on his face deepened. "How's that winning?"

It was the very essence of winning. Hooking her arm through his, she steered him toward the elevator.

People in the lobby looked at them oddly. His unbuttoned shirt, stained and torn beneath his soft black leather jacket, was enough cause for hotel guests to move out of his way as he passed. The way they would for any thug or danger to society.

It occurred to her that although she knew what Cole did for a living now, the man's life had huge gaps and he was essentially a stranger to her. Questions were breeding questions inside her head.

"I got him to stop treating me as if I was twelve and in need of supervision." Reaching the elevator bank, she pressed for a car. The doors opened almost instantly. She looked at him. "Now let's get you to your room and see about cleaning up the scar in the making." Because he was waiting, she walked in ahead of him. Nice to know his manners went deep. "And for your information, scars aren't sexy."

He tried to smile and found his mouth was too sore to complete the movement. He forced it to his lips despite the pain. He couldn't resist looking at her for a long, languid moment. Right now, it was the highlight of a very bad day.

"That all depends on who's wearing them and where they are," he said.

She decided that it was in her best interest not to touch the remark.

They reached his room within less than two minutes. Though she'd placed herself almost against him once the doors opened again, an open, silent invitation to lean on her, Cole made the trip from elevator to room on his own power.

Rayne was quick to take inventory of the small medicine cabinet. It was stocked with everything involved with cleanliness.

"There's nothing in here," she announced in disgust, slamming the mirrored door shut.

That didn't surprise him. He lowered himself onto the bed slowly. Cole could feel his bones groaning. He was going to feel like hell tomorrow.

"I don't imagine hotels figure you'll get into a car accident, or a fight," he said. According to the reflection he saw in the mirrored wardrobe door, he looked like he came back from battle.

She frowned at him. "Still say you should go to the hospital."

"It's a cut. My head is still attached, although right about now, I'm kind of wishing it weren't." He didn't give in to the temptation to hold it. That way only lay more pain. He saw her heading for the door. "Going home?"

Why did he want to get rid of her so badly? Rayne asked herself. Was it because he didn't want her witnessing his pain, or was there some other reason he kept suggesting she leave? "Going to the pharmacy," she corrected. She pinned him with a look. "You stay put."

She didn't have to tell him twice. He was vaguely aware of the door closing as he stretched out on the bed.

* * *

Walking in a few minutes later, Rayne found her would-be patient lying on the bed, his eyes closed. She recalled something about it being dangerous to fall asleep just after sustaining a head wound.

Panic reared its head, materializing out of the darkness, assaulting her. Still clutching the small brown bag she'd picked up at the hotel pharmacy in one hand, she felt for his pulse with the other.

Nothing. Dropping the bag, she began feeling around different regions on his wrist, trying to discern any sort of faint rhythm.

Cole's eyes fluttered open and then he was looking at her with those big, blue eyes of his. Eyes that held more than a hint of amusement in them. "You could just as easily hold up a mirror to my nose to see if I was breathing."

She blew out a breath, not at all happy about the amount of relief she was experiencing. "Couldn't manage to rip it off the wall."

With effort, he raised himself up into a sitting position. The room spun a little as he fiercely tried to pin it in place.

"You don't carry a mirror with you?"

"Don't need one." Taking off her shoulder strap, Rayne threw her purse onto the chair. She shook her head. "I know what I look like." She shrugged. "For the most part, anyway."

He watched as she emptied the paper sack she'd picked up at the hotel pharmacy on the bed. A box of butterfly Band-Aids, a small bottle of peroxide and a bag of cotton balls came tumbling out.

"How about that, a woman who's not vain. That's something of a rarity."

She went over to the sink to wash her hands. "You've been hanging around the wrong women."

"No, that's Eric's dilemma." He raised his voice a little to be heard above the running water. It echoed wildly in his head, and he lowered it again. "I haven't been hanging around women at all. At least, not single ones."

Opening up the bag of cotton balls, she doused one with peroxide, then dabbed it against his forehead and watched as he winced.

"Married women?"

Was he like his father, after all? She'd heard rumors about the senior Garrison's lifestyle. It was one of those secrets everyone knew about. Lyle Garrison liked variety.

Wasn't peroxide not supposed to sting? Cole found he had to struggle not to make a sound. He wouldn't have put it past her to have slipped some alcohol into the bottle just to get even with him because he'd wanted her to drop her part in the investigation. But that had been strictly for her own safety. He didn't want to be responsible for anything happening to her.

"It's not what you think." His eyes fluttered shut for a second as he felt her working over him, her cool fingers brushing against his forehead. "The women are married, but they're part of the families who move into the houses my company refurbishes."

"'Homes for the homeless,' isn't that your slogan?"

The project encompassed far more than that. "Except that we lump anyone who's never had a home into that." The idea had taken seed several years ago, while watching a commercial regarding mortgages of all things. The first-time buyer looked elated to be moving from a crammed apartment to a place that had its own yard, however small. Cole realized he wanted to see that expression on someone's face firsthand.

"Everyone should be able to own their own home."

Taking a Band-Aid out of the box, she carefully opened the sterile wrapping. "Very noble."

The slight pressure made his head spin more. It was hard to keep in focus. "I don't know if it's noble, but it's practical."

The man was modest. Who would have thought a Garrison was capable of being modest? she thought. "It's 'more practical' dealing in expensive mansions and making a ton of money."

He raised a shoulder carelessly, then winced as pain shot through it as he dropped it again. Maybe he should soak in a hot tub. "I don't need a ton of money. And despite what my parents believe, not every success is measured in dollars and cents."

"Like I said, very noble." Finished, she stood back and looked at her handiwork. Not bad.

She still would have rather that Cole had listened to her and gone to the hospital, but she understood why he didn't. She probably would have been just as stubborn in his place.

Setting the Band-Aid box aside, she took his chin in her hand and examined his eye. More than a little hint of color was setting in. The bruising just made him look that much more rakish. "You're going to have a shiner, but there's nothing I can do about that."

When she took her hand away, he found himself wishing that she hadn't. "You could order a steak."

She put the medical supplies in the bathroom. Her voice floated back out to him. "I don't know if room service would send up a raw steak."

"I was thinking of medium rare." She came out of the bathroom to look at him. "Big enough for two. You haven't eaten, either," he reminded her.

She was tempted. But if she remained any longer, it wouldn't be to partake of a steak and she knew it.

They both knew it.

"No, I'd better get going." She picked up her purse and slipped the strap over her shoulder. "I did a little more nosing around at the precinct and there are a couple of things I want to check out."

"Such as?" He began to rise to his feet.

Very gently she pushed him back down on the bed. "I used the singular, not the plural. 'I' not 'we.' You get some rest."

"It's my brother," he protested. And head injury or not, they were running out of time. And maybe stumbling onto something. Why else would someone have tampered with his car?

She banked down her impatience. He had to listen to reason. "But we're doing things my way, remember? That means I get to make the rules and you get to listen to them. Tonight's rule says you stay here, get some rest, and we'll hook up in the morning."

Maybe it was for the best. He wasn't much good to anyone in his present condition. "I'll pick you up at eight."

"In what? Your car's been totaled, remember? I'll pick you up," she told him. "Want to do something useful tonight, call the rental company and see if you can get a car for yourself."

He supposed that was something. "And you're going home?"

"I'm going home." She was eager to get her hands on a computer and hack into the department's database to find out exactly who was at the precinct during the time that Cole was there. Not that anyone couldn't have come in from the outside and sabotaged his car, but it was more likely someone from within the department had done it. Which both upset her and made her blood run cold. "Don't look so concerned."

"I don't trust you."

"Well, you're going to have to." She patted his cheek. The contact seeped into her consciousness. She dropped her hand. "Besides, this time, I'm telling the truth. Now get some rest. You look terrible."

He got to his feet. "You do know how to turn a guy's head, don't you?"

She felt a little overwhelmed by his presence. All the excitement was taking its toll, using up whatever spare air existed in the room. "You wouldn't need too much head turning. You look dizzy."

"I guess I am, a little." And it was getting worse, not better, but not for the reason he knew she thought. Cole slipped his fingers into her hair, his palm brushing against her cheek. "Seeing as how I'm already dizzy, I don't figure I've got anything to lose anyway—"

"What?" The single word got stuck in her throat, lodged there by her breath. Neither was going anywhere.

"Nothing." He wasn't making any sense. Nothing was making any sense. Except that he wanted to kiss her.

Chapter 11

*Y*es!

No!

The protest echoed in her head, coming with lightning speed on the heels of the affirmation.

She shouldn't be doing this. He shouldn't be doing this. They were trying to prove his brother innocent, they needed clear heads, not hot bodies. This only muddied the waters, blurred the borders of their relationship and what they were trying to accomplish. She was after the truth and if she made love with him, that put her in danger of making her prejudice in his favor.

Hell, she'd always been prejudiced in his favor.

It had nothing to do with the murder, or his brother, or anything beyond one spirit finally finding the other. Kindred spirits, that's what he'd called the two of them, and deep down, some part of her had always felt that they were.

Air, she needed air.

Brain functions ceased when there was no air and she clearly wasn't thinking. Not with her head, anyway.

With effort, Rayne put her hands on his chest, hands that could so easily wrap themselves around his neck instead, and pushed, managing to create a small wedge between them.

He looked at her, his eyes slightly dazed. Because of the accident? Or because she'd pushed him away? "I'm sorry," he finally said.

The words stung. They shouldn't have. She'd been the one to stop this. It took her a second to get her tongue in working order. "Are you?"

His eyes studied her, looking for answers, for clues. "I am if you are."

So that was it, he was trying not to offend her. They'd gone way past that, into a region where there were no offenses, no insults, only needs. And she was having trouble finding her way back.

She took a breath to steady herself. It didn't really help. "I'm not, but this isn't exactly the prescribed method of treatment after a car accident."

Cole blinked. "What car accident?" He saw the concern that immediately leaped into her eyes and instantly felt guilty. "I'm kidding." His arms tightened around her just a shade, but he refrained from lowering his mouth back down to hers. This was going to be mutual or it wasn't going to be at all. "If this isn't the prescribed treatment, it should be.'' But she could have other reasons, legitimate reasons, for not wanting him to do this. Cole held himself in check even when everything screamed for him to continue. ''Am I invading your space?''

''No, but I'm hopeful.'' Damn it, it wasn't the right thing to say, the right thing to do, but she couldn't help herself. She wanted him. Wanted him badly. And there was no way she could make herself withdraw.

Talk about mixed signals. Cole tried to read hers, tried to separate what she wanted from what he wanted. Was he reading things into this, things he wanted to see? ''I don't want to compromise you—''

Enough. She could only be so noble, so righteous. Every nerve ending in her body had gone on the alert, waiting. Wanting.

The hell with everything, she thought. At this moment, this felt right.

She ran her tongue along her lips. They remained dry. Thirsting for him. Her heart pounded within her chest as she began to unbutton his shirt.

''Right now, truth be told, I'd like nothing more than to be compromised.'' And then she grinned that funny little half smile of hers that shot itself straight to his gut. ''I guess that's a little too honest, isn't it?''

His eyes on hers, looking for some signal that told him to stop, Cole began to move her jacket off her shoulders, down her arms. ''Honest is good. I always liked honest. It's games I never cared for.''

She yanked the shirttails out of his waistband. He unbuckled her holster. Her grin widened even as desire tightened its hold on her. "Amazing how much we have in common."

Very carefully, holding on to the hilt of her revolver, he removed her gun and holster from her. Instead of tossing it the way she did his shirt, he handed the weapon to her. "Amazing."

Her breath shortened the instant she placed the weapon down on the table by the bed. Cole began to unbutton her blouse, an urgency moving through his fingers, increasing his speed. His fingers brushed against her skin as they moved, enticing her.

Rayne felt as if she were engaged in a session of strip poker, except that no cards were involved, no hands won and lost. There were no losers right now, only winners, because she could sense that he wanted this as much as she did.

And she wanted it very, very much.

Rayne sucked in her breath as he unbuttoned her slacks. Her body warmed as she did the same for him. As if in unison, they each guided the material away, sending clothing falling to the floor as flames were fanned, growing ever higher.

She felt him step out of his shoes. She stayed in hers a second longer. There was nothing else between them but heat.

Cole sealed his mouth to hers, hardly knowing what he was doing. He'd reverted to automatic pilot, allowing his body to take the lead. Because his mind was utterly mesmerized.

It wasn't the accident that caused his head to spin so badly, to create that wild rushing noise in his ears.

It was the fact that his blood had heated to an almost astronomical degree and would continue heating until he had this woman, had her utterly and completely in the most physical sense of the word.

It was as if a sudden, undeniable craving had hit him and only she would sate it.

With the last of her clothing peeled away, his hands warmed her skin, heating him even more as he committed the outline of her body to tactile memory. She felt small, delicate, something he knew was a complete fallacy.

Lorrayne Cavanaugh was the strongest woman he had ever met in his life.

The contradiction excited him.

She excited him.

It occurred to him, even as he lost himself in the warmth of her, that he hadn't felt like this in a very long time. Somewhere along the journey of his life, he'd become convinced that he'd lost the ability to feel anything at all.

He'd been wrong.

The daily business of living had somehow pushed these kinds of emotions out of his realm of existence. And he was all right with that. But he was far better with this. With the soft, supple feel of skin against skin, with the imprisoning feel of heat emanating from her loins, seeking him out. Bringing him to his knees.

He couldn't get enough of her.

He wanted to try.

His lips raced over her face, her throat, her shoulders, her breasts. Each place he touched seemed to ignite. Rayne felt herself falling into a frenzy of feelings.

She had no idea how they wound up on his bed, had no idea where she was, or even who. All that had fled from her head.

All she knew was that there was a flame inside of her and it had to be fed, had to continue. She wanted to bathe in it forever.

Urges slammed through her, begging for release. She felt dangerously close to exploding. Bodies wrapped together, she cleaved to his, trying to absorb every sensation as it passed over her.

His hands were as skillful as his lips, bringing her up to dizzying heights of delicious sensations so effortlessly, so quickly, it stole her breath away. As if she ever had it.

The first explosion came when desire rushed up and over a peak Rayne hadn't even realized was looming in front of her.

She cried out, the sound rumbling into his mouth as he kissed her. She felt him pause, as if in wonder, and then resume the fine rhythm of his body brushing up against hers.

Just skin to skin, no union. But that was coming. Her body was pleading for it.

Damn, but it was hard keeping himself in check when all he wanted was to push himself into her, to lose himself inside of her. To have that release that every fiber of his body was begging for.

But the pleasure of having her so completely his

both excited and humbled him and it was worth the bittersweet sacrifice of waiting.

Every kiss, every touch, while building to the final climax, seemed to have a life of its own and wrapped him up in it. His pulse raced so fast he was surprised it hadn't burst out of his body.

Cole feasted on what she had to offer him, becoming intimately familiar with every part of her, from her toes on up and then back down again, anointing all of her. Bringing her up to the very pinnacle of a climax time and again. Reveling in the way she twisted and turned against him, savoring the tastes that met his tongue.

He felt as if he had never made love before. At least, not this completely.

Her body slick with desire, she shivered as he made his path down past her belly. Promising another sharp jolt through her body. But she wanted him there with her, wanted him to feel that same wild ride that she did. She wanted that final union.

Rayne tangled her fingers in his hair, exhausted. With strength that came from somewhere beyond her understanding, she dragged Cole back up along her body, her core throbbing violently, from the feel of his mouth, from anticipation of what was to come.

"Damn it," she cried hoarsely as she looked up into the face that loomed over her, "I'm going to arrest you if you don't—"

"Can't have that—" He laughed softly, though the words had entered his mouth through something that was beyond the scope of his power.

The time had come. He couldn't hold back another moment, even if the fate of the world depended on it. It wasn't physically possible.

His face over hers, he took the open invitation her raised hips gave and slipped inside of her.

The small noise that escaped her lips almost drove him wild.

The rhythm was not slow. It was almost mach speed from the very beginning, increasing ever faster with each frantic beat of their hearts that were pressed against one another. And then his arms tightened around her, as if he meant to pull her into him.

Amid the turbulence, something fell into place inside of her. She felt whole.

The explosion came, taking them both into its center. Catapulting them both to a grassy plane where an incredible sense of peace and euphoria found them, if only for a moment. A moment was still longer than either one of them had anticipated.

She was never going to get her breath back again, Rayne thought. There wasn't enough air available to accomplish that.

Her head was spinning badly as she tried to get her bearings. They kept slipping away from her, rolling just out of reach. She felt like someone trying to fight off the effects of anesthesia. Not altogether sure she wanted to. Waking up had consequences that she wasn't sure she wanted to face.

Still fighting for air, Rayne ran her tongue along her lips. They were parched, dry. But she could still taste him.

A thrill ran over her; she tried vainly to hold it at bay without much luck. Slowly, reality came drifting back. She'd just made love with a man who could just as easily been killed less than an hour ago. She should be taking him to a hospital in her car, not trying to put him into one via gymnastics. Guilt raised its hoary head, shooting pointy quills at her.

She turned her head just a fraction to look at him. "You all right?"

Very slowly, Cole rolled off her, then gathered her into the crook of his arm. She was rewarded with a smile. "I dunno. I might never be the same again."

She wasn't fishing for a compliment, just an answer. "I mean, what we just did, that didn't mess up your condition?"

Damn it, her tongue felt fat, unwieldy. She couldn't find the right words.

"Oh, I wouldn't put it that way." Had he really given this any thought, he knew he would have found it unsettling. But for now, he decided just to enjoy it. "I think I'm very badly messed up."

Concern leaped into her veins. What had she been thinking, letting her needs get the better of her? For all she knew, the man could have a concussion, internal bleeding, or even worse. "Should I take you to the hospital?"

He let his eyes travel over as much as he was about to take in at this vantage point. The police detective had one killer of a body.

"And make all the doctors jealous?" Turning his

body into hers, he let his fingers strum along her skin. "What good would that do?"

A compliment, he was giving her a compliment. Rayne had no idea something so simple could touch her that much. She found herself smiling even as she tried to be serious. "I mean, you were in an accident. Maybe what we just did, what I just did," she corrected, annoyed with her own lack of restraint, "put you in some kind of jeopardy."

Yes, there was jeopardy, but it wasn't the kind she was thinking of. He tried not to think about it. Instead, he grinned and winked at her, making the pit of her stomach flutter in response. "What a way to go."

She struggled to remember that what they'd just done could have major repercussions and not that she wanted to do it all again. Rayne blew out a breath in a heated huff. "Cole, I'm not kidding."

Watching her chest rise and fall, Cole felt the hunger beginning anew. As incredible as it was, he wanted her again, even though he thought that there was no way he could. At least, he'd never wanted a woman he'd just had before. Once, a good once, was usually his limit.

Usually.

But not tonight.

He reached for her, bringing her back to his level again, nestling her against him. Surprising himself at the incredible feeling of well-being that was seeping over him, a feeling he was hard-pressed to remember ever having experienced before.

"Shh," he coaxed. "Just relax."

Relax was the last thing she could do. All her nerves were on alert again, standing at attention, ready to dive into action.

Ready to be set on fire again.

She wanted to pull him down on her, to merge their bodies again and to hold on to the fire with her bare hands. "Easy for you to say, you're not lying next to a naked man."

This time the grin threatened to split his face in two. "No," he conceded, "I'm not. But there is this amazing naked woman beside me and I'm having a very hard time…"

Her eyes slid down along his belly, dipping lower. The smile that took her lips was sly, and very, very pleased.

Her arms entwined themselves around his neck. "Are you, now?"

He laughed, his arm tightening around her as he brought her ever closer. So close that she was almost a part of him.

"Yes," he whispered against her skin, brushing a wreath of kisses along it, "I am. Don't let me have it alone."

Rayne pulled her head back just a little, her eyes finding his. "Wouldn't be very hospitable of me, would it?"

He moved his head from side to side, his eyes never leaving hers. He stirred things inside of her, things she couldn't begin to untangle and name. Things part of her was afraid to untangle and name. If there was no name, there could be no marker for it when it died and left her, as she knew it had to.

"'Fraid not," he told her.

Her head raised, she kissed each corner of his mouth, then lay back again. Temptation served hot. "So what is it you want me to do?"

His hand cupped her cheek as his eyes caressed every part of her. He'd branded her and for tonight, for now, she was his. "Guess."

Surprising him, she pushed Cole back onto the bed. With her hand resting on his chest, Rayne lightly brushed her lips against his. Quickening his pulse, hardening his desire. Evidence of both throbbed against her. Making her smile as she pulled back her head just a little to look at him.

"So, am I on the right track?"

"You are." She kissed him again, bringing his desire to full fruition. "Damn, but you are," he murmured.

Cole dove his fingers into her hair, cupping the back of her head, pulling her even closer to him. Carefully, he moved her so that her body was on top of his. So that he could feel every subtle nuance, every fiber of her being against him.

Her heart racing, she pulled her head away for a moment. It was all the time she felt she could spare. "Good, I'd hate to be in the wrong place."

"Never happen," he told her just before he framed her face, bringing her mouth down to his again.

She forgot all about bringing him to the hospital.

*   *   *

"You didn't come home last night."

Her hand on the doorknob of the back entrance, Rayne froze. Slowly her heels met the floor. There was no point in tiptoeing in, not when her father was standing right here in the kitchen. It was a good half hour before she knew he normally got started.

Damn it, the one morning she needed him to stick to his schedule, he'd gone for free-form.

With a shrug, she closed the door behind her. He'd had his back to her when he'd sent the remark in her direction and she looked at it now. Had he waited up for her? Or just gotten up and checked her room before coming down?

Had he worried? She didn't want him worrying. But she was a grown woman now and shouldn't have to submit to a verbal questionnaire just because she hadn't filled out a form in triplicate, citing exactly where she'd be for the night.

When he turned to look at her over his shoulder, she gave him what she hoped passed for an innocent look. "No, I didn't."

He turned back to the cabinet beneath the counter, taking out the first of a host of pans. "Long time since you've felt the need to sneak in."

He was right. She'd reverted back to behavior she'd exhibited as a teen. Staying out all hours, coming home in the morning, hoping to get lost in the crowd.

As if.

To her father, each of the Cavanaugh children was

an individual and he kept track of them all as such. That included their comings and goings.

Rayne looked away. ''Just working on a case,'' she told him evasively.

''A case of what?'' He opened the refrigerator and took out a carton of orange juice. He poured two glasses, handing the first to her. Surprised, she took it from him. ''You're on vacation, remember?''

No, she hadn't remembered. This ''vacation'' thing was hard to get accustomed to. It also left her without an alibi. She put the half-empty glass on the counter, digging in. ''Dad, I'm too old for this.''

Again, he surprised her. ''Yes, you are. You're your own woman now.'' He laughed shortly, shaking his head. ''You always were, straight from the womb.'' Taking out a loaf of bread, he moved it to the side to make room for a box of waffle mix. ''But that doesn't mean you always know what you're doing.'' There was a pregnant pause in the air. Andrew turned to look at his youngest daughter. ''*Do* you know what you're doing, Rayne?''

If he'd approached it in any other way, she would have brazened it out, declared yes she knew what she was doing and saying so in no uncertain terms just before she stormed out of the kitchen.

But the look in her father's eyes, kind, understanding, sympathetic, completely unlaced her resolve. She couldn't get angry if he wasn't challenging her, wasn't telling her what to do. He was treating her like an adult and this fact took away her greatest weapon, her anger.

She knew what she was doing when it came to

Eric's case. She was looking for the truth. But as far as what was happening between her and Cole, she hadn't a clue. "I think so."

Andrew nodded as he took out a large mixing bowl. "Okay, then, I'll back you." Putting the bowl on the counter, he looked at her. "Whatever you need, you got it, you know that."

She smiled. No matter what he said to the contrary, she knew her father was in her corner. That was just the way he was. "Yes, I know that."

He crossed to her, worried the way only a loving father could be. "But be careful, Rayne, be very careful. Don't step on the wrong toes."

She held up her hand as if she was taking a pledge. "Just the bad guys, Dad."

No one told them about this part, Andrew thought, when they became parents. No one said that from that day forward, even the best of days would contain a nugget of concern, of worry burrowed into it. It was just the way things were.

He nodded toward the counter with its array of ingredients waiting to be turned into something tempting. "Hungry?"

She grinned. "I could eat."

Andrew gestured toward the table as he crossed to the stove. "Then sit down. Be nice having you the first one at the table for a change instead of the last."

Taking a seat, Rayne smiled to herself. "Yes, Dad."

Chapter 12

Rayne frowned at the cell phone in the palm of her hand. She'd just snapped it closed.

That was the third one.

The third time someone had called to warn her off the investigation. Each warning was a little more harsh, a little more graphic in its threat. This one had known exactly where to hit. This one had threatened her family.

"What is it?" Cole wanted to know. He'd already asked her once, but she'd said nothing in reply. Concern began eating away at him and he debated pulling off onto the shoulder of the road to conduct a deeper inquiry. But the clock in his head continued ticking, diminishing the minutes his brother had left before the trial. He kept driving.

''Rayne, what is it?'' There was no mistaking the demand in his voice.

She looked at him as if she were coming out of a daze, her mind vibrating, jumping from thought to thought, trying to sort things out. Trying to put things into perspective.

It had been two days since they'd initially made love. Two days in which they'd alternated between ignoring the elephant in the living room and assuming a kind of tense truce between them, a truce that had its share of isolated, intimate glances, intimate touches, all of which fled almost faster than they materialized.

It wasn't a comfortable place to be, but then, she'd never gravitated toward the comfortable, the complacent. That wasn't her style.

And she had a feeling that it wasn't his.

Throughout it all, she tried to keep the case involving his brother paramount. After all, there was a life at stake, not just a heart, or whatever it was that she felt was at risk in her private world. But now that same case was threatening what she held most dear. Her father, her siblings.

Her back stiffened.

''Who was on the phone?'' Cole pressed. He wasn't about to be put off.

''I don't know.'' Frustration clawed at her. ''The same person who called before.''

''Anything new?'' He knew the answer to that before he asked. Her expression had gone flat.

''Yeah.'' She pushed out the word on a long breath.

"There's something new." She looked at him. "Mr. Metal Voice threatened my family."

"Which means we *are* getting close to something." Cole slanted a glance at her before looking back to the road. This was his fight, not hers. He couldn't ask her to put anyone in her family in jeopardy for him, even if they were all part of the police department. "I'll take you home."

There was too much traffic for him to switch lanes to get in the extreme left-hand side to make a U-turn, but he could probably manage it by the end of the next long block.

But Rayne shook her head. "Date's not over yet, Romeo. Just keep going the way you were going. We've got a full day ahead of us."

Cole stole another glance. He wasn't convinced yet. "But—"

"I've made up my mind. Nobody threatens the Cavanaughs." As soon as she said it, she knew it sounded like something out of a grade B Western, but it didn't make it any less the truth. They'd all sworn to uphold the law, every last one of them. There were consequences to that oath, but that didn't stop them from taking it. From believing in it. It's what made them what they were. "We can take care of ourselves."

Damn it, who did she think she was, John Wayne? "Rayne—"

She wasn't about to have him try to argue her out of it. She'd known the risks when she'd started this, had known them better than he did.

"Look, someone's cut your brake lines, someone's been playing dial-a-threat with me. And—" she glanced up into the rearview mirror "—if I'm not mistaken, someone's been following us ever since you pulled out of the hotel parking lot."

His eyes darted up to the mirror. Two vehicles lurked behind them. The white sports car directly behind them did not look familiar, but the beige car trailing after it was the typical kind of car used for surveillance work.

Cole was sure, now that he thought of it, that he'd seen the car pulling out after them when he'd left the hotel parking lot. But was he letting the situation get to him and becoming paranoid? The beige car could very well just be a coincidence.

Gut instinct told him that it wasn't.

They were on their way out of town, traveling to a small town located up the coast. Bainbridge-by-the-sea. The man who lived in the apartment directly above Kathy Fallon's, Matthew Klein, still hadn't returned home so they couldn't question him. He'd been gone since the day after he'd given his initial statement to the police. The woman at the apartment complex's rental office had reluctantly given them the name of Klein's employer who in turn had told them that Matthew Klein had taken an unexpected vacation.

It went a long way toward fueling Cole's suspicions. Had the man seen something? Was he in fear for his life? Rayne had to agree that the scenario wasn't nearly as farfetched as it sounded. Covertly tapping into the phone company's records had allowed her to discover that Klein had made reservations at a bed-and-breakfast inn located up the coast.

"If he's fleeing for his life," she'd commented to Cole after making the discovery, "he's certainly doing it in a novel fashion."

They were driving toward Bainbridge-by-the-sea now.

Was the beige car going there, as well?

Turning back around in her seat, Rayne looked at Cole. She was willing to bet the man had more than one trick up his sleeve, and more than one good twist. More than that, she was counting on it. "Are you up to some fancy driving?"

He seemed to read her mind. If she had any doubts, the smile he gave her erased them. Gripping the wheel, he advised, "Just hold on to your seat."

She'd rather that he hold on to it, but kept the thought to herself. Now wasn't the time.

That it might never be the time was something she would deal with later.

With the aplomb of someone with several defensive driving courses under his belt, Cole took twists and turns through the northern end of town that would have left a racer breathless. Rayne kept one eye open for the local police, but no squad car appeared, no bright dancing lights shadowed their journey as they detoured off their route several times before finally managing to lose the beige sedan.

It had taken them the better part of forty minutes, but it was well worth it.

"Where the hell did you learn how to drive like that?"

He thought of Bogota, of driving while guerrillas shelled the vehicle from all sides. It was the closest he'd come to being part of a miracle.

Until the other night, a voice inside him whispered. He ignored it.

"A story for another time," was all he told her.

She wasn't about to let him off the hook that easily. "I'll look forward to it."

Cole saw the shadow of a diner up on the road ahead of them. He felt as if he were running on empty. A good strong cup of coffee would go a long way to filling that space. The diner was approximately twenty feet away from the freeway on-ramp. He'd be willing to bet whoever ran it made a nice piece of change on the through traffic.

"You want to stop for something to eat?" He began slowing the vehicle, a rental he'd gotten at the hotel, anticipating her answer. He already knew what his was.

Rayne flashed a grin. "Always."

"Always it is." Making a right turn, he drove toward the diner and eased the car into one of the three last available spaces. Getting out, he glanced around the dirt-lined lot. For an off hour, the diner seemed to be doing brisk business.

Brisk was also a good way to describe the wind as it followed them inside the diner. Rayne unbuttoned her jacket, but left it on.

She wasn't sure just when she actually became

aware of it. Whether it was immediately upon entering the diner or on hearing the voice of the woman behind the counter. Or when she looked up into the waitress's face. Looking back, she definitely felt as if she'd stepped through some kind of looking glass, not knowing what it was that made this moment different from all the moments that had come before, only that something *was* very, very different and would continue to be that way from this day forward.

At first, her thoughts were completely centered on the beige car and the wild-goose chase they'd just led it on. They progressed without ceremony onto the unsettling cell call with its blunt threat. Had her brain not been in a million different places at once, it would have honed in on the feeling instantly rather than several beats later.

But it was there, unmistakably.

One minute her thoughts went elsewhere, the next, they had inexplicably leaped back to her father and his never-ending and unrealistic quest to find her mother.

Maybe it was because she'd glanced at the photograph of her mother before she'd left the house that morning.

Or maybe it was something else.

All she knew was that she was suddenly looking into the face of a person who, had she not known better, Rayne would have sworn was her mother. Not the way Rose Cavanaugh had looked that last day she had seen her alive, but the way her mother would have looked now, with fifteen years accrued between visits.

The full impact didn't hit Rayne until she was

seated at the counter beside Cole and the woman
sailed by, a coffeepot in her hand, on her way to refill
several cups. As she moved passed them, the waitress
dealt out two plastic menus along with a flash of a
smile that she shot in their direction.

It was the smile that did it, that triggered the mem-
ories.

Her mother smiled like that. Quick, bright, one side
higher than the other.

"You know, you're getting positively spooky,"
Cole told her, keeping his voice down. He'd been talking to her for about two minutes without any indication from Rayne that she'd heard a word of it. "That's
the second time you've spaced out on me this morning." He leaned his head into hers. "You see someone?"

She couldn't take her eyes off the woman, searching
for similarities beyond the strange feeling that made
her heart stop. "Yes."

As covertly as possible, Cole looked around the
small diner. There were more than the usual handful
of truckers mixed in with an elderly couple talking
earnestly in a booth and another booth occupied by
two parents obviously on vacation with their three
children, all under the age of seven. The parents
looked ready to surrender.

"Who?" He dropped his voice down to a whisper.
And then he saw that Rayne's eyes were riveted on
the waitress. "You know her?"

Rayne pressed her lips together. Doubt warred with

certainty that had no roots, no foundation. Just an unshakable feeling.

"Maybe," she murmured, then raised her voice. "Excuse me." The woman, still holding the pot of coffee, turned in her direction. Her inquiring smile caused something strange to tug at Rayne's emotions.

Maybe she was just stressed out, she tried to tell herself.

It was a lie and she knew it.

"Yes, honey?"

The voice, even the voice was the same. It seemed to echo back to her from the past.

Was she going crazy?

As the woman crossed to her, Rayne looked at the name tag that was pinned jauntily to the waitress's blue uniform. It told her the woman's name was "Claire."

Vaguely aware that Cole was watching her, Rayne took her first hesitant steps across the tightrope. "Are you by any chance related to the Cavanaughs?"

"Cavanaugh, Cavanaugh…" The woman called Claire rolled the name on her tongue, as if tasting it first to see if it was bitter or sweet. And then she smiled again as she shook her head, dark blond curls swaying around her heart-shaped face. "Nope, can't say I know them." Another smile came and went, like sunshine rolling along the plains. "Wish I could help." The waitress held up the pot in her hand, her eyes moving from Cole's face to hers. "How about some coffee?"

Rayne was vaguely aware of numbly nodding her head.

Cole waited until the woman moved away again. "Rayne, what the hell is going on here?"

She wanted to tell him, to have the words come pouring out. But what if she was wrong? What if whatever fever had caused her father to hang on to hope all these years had become infectious? What if she'd caught it, too? She didn't relish looking like an idiot. Not without some kind of proof to offer beyond a feeling in the pit of her stomach.

"Nothing." Turning her stool in the opposite direction, she slipped off. "Excuse me for a second." Before Cole could ask her where she was going, she made her way over to the older woman seated at the cash register on the opposite end of the diner.

The woman looked up from the book she was reading, her expression quizzical.

She had questions, however absurd, that needed answering. But because they were so strange, she didn't want to ask them where she could be overheard. When she saw Cole begin to follow her, Rayne waved him back to his stool, then waited until he complied before turning back to the cashier.

"Cute little thing," Claire commented, filling his cup. "You two together?"

"What? No, just here on business," Cole said, watching Rayne, wondering what she was up to.

"You should always make time for a little pleasure," the woman told him. "Life goes by too quickly."

She had a point, he thought. But right now there wasn't very much he could do about it. He took a sip of the inky liquid, letting it work through his senses. Rayne was back before he had a chance to finish. "What was all that about?"

Her heart was still racing. What she'd found out had raised more questions, questions that didn't have any immediate answers. But they reinforced her initial feelings.

"Just checking something out." She saw the way he looked at her. "About another case," she added, "not your brother's." She wasn't any more forthcoming than that.

It grated on his nerves, even as he told himself that if it was about another case, she had every right to keep it to herself. All he cared about was what concerned his brother.

It didn't quite ring true. For better or worse, she had been added to the mix.

They ordered and ate a light brunch. He noted that Rayne spent the remainder of the time looking at the waitress. It took effort to keep his questions to himself, but he knew that in her place, he would have appreciated it.

After an hour's drive up a coast that was generally hospitable as far as the weather went, they finally arrived at the bed-and-breakfast where Matthew Klein had booked a room.

In this case, "quaint" was a euphemism for old and

badly in need of new paint, but on the whole, there was a charm to the seventy-five-year-old building.

"I wouldn't mind staying at a place like this my-self," Rayne said. The comment arose out of a sudden need to get away from everything, to find a space where she could just think without feeling as if she were in the midst of putting out fires.

"Why don't you?" he asked, holding the front door open for her. "Once this is all over?"

She noticed that he didn't expand the suggestion to include both of them, but then, she didn't need him in order to relax, she told herself. With him around, she probably *couldn't* relax.

"Maybe I will," she murmured.

With the help of the man at the front desk, they found Matthew Klein and his girlfriend in the dining room. They were sitting with their heads together, sharing a moment, sharing a laugh.

"He doesn't look like a man who'd welcome un-expected company, however brief," Cole commented.

"Then we won't stay too long," Rayne said over her shoulder.

Cole's assessment was right on the nose. Matthew Klein was far from happy about the interruption once Rayne had shown him her badge. He threw down his napkin on the table and rose to his feet, moving to the side. Forcing Rayne and Cole to do the same. It was obvious he didn't want his girlfriend to find out about the grisly murder that had taken place a few feet away from him.

"Look, I already gave a statement. If you don't

mind, I'd like to put the whole gruesome thing behind me." To prove his point, he added, "I'm moving out as of the first of the month."

The nature of her work had made suspicion second nature. "Rather sudden, isn't it?"

Klein's dark brows narrowed over darker eyes. "So was the murder."

She didn't want to alienate the man. They'd questioned everyone else in the complex, Klein was their last hope as far as trying to validate Cole's theory that there was another man in the picture somehow. Rayne looked at him with renewed interest. Could *he* have had something to do with Kathy Fallon's murder?

"Is there anything else you can tell us, anything at all that comes to mind?" Rayne prodded.

Cole asked the only question that mattered to him. "Was she seeing anyone else?"

"No." Klein made no attempt to hide his annoyance. He glanced back at his girlfriend and waved to her. The expression on his face when he turned back toward them made Cole think of Dr. Jekyll and Mr. Hyde. "I already said all this. The only guy I ever saw coming and going from her place was that cop." Klein shrugged dismissively. "I figure he was there to protect her." And then he frowned. "Didn't do a very good job of it, did he?"

Rayne's attention had been snared. "What do you mean, protect her?"

Her question earned her a stare, as if they weren't really communicating in the same language. "I saw him coming around a lot."

"And nobody else?" Cole pressed.

Klein's head rotated like a top, from Rayne back to him. "No."

"What do you mean by 'a lot'?" Rayne asked. She wasn't sure if it was wishful thinking that had her feeling maybe, just maybe, they'd finally stumbled onto something. Maybe that was why she was being warned off the way she was. Maybe there was a cop involved.

Klein's patience gave every impression of wearing thin. He lifted his wide shoulders, then let them drop again. "I dunno. Five, six times, maybe more. A lot, okay? Our paths kept crossing," he explained. "Now if you don't mind—" he began to turn away from them "—I was about to propose—"

But Rayne caught hold of his shoulder. "One more thing."

She was playing a hunch, but that was what good police work was, ninety percent sweat and hard work and ten percent luck. It was the luck that carried them.

Taking out her wallet, she flipped to a group photograph that had been taken at her father's old partner's retirement party a couple of months ago. She held it up for Klein's perusal now. "Do you see him in this picture?"

Disgruntled, Klein took her wallet in his hand and stared at the cluster of police personnel. "No."

"Are you sure?"

"I said no, didn't I?" he demanded. But then, just as she took back her wallet, he caught her hand. "Wait, let me look at that again." Taking the wallet

back, Klein stared at the photograph she'd held up.
"Him." He pointed to the man in the center of the
group. "I remember because the first time I saw him,
he looked so tall to me. I thought he might hit his
head on the doorway when he went into her apartment." He handed the wallet back. "Okay?"

She didn't hear his question.

Longwell, she thought. Kathy Fallon's neighbor had
just picked out Longwell.

Feeling slightly numb, slightly excited, she slipped
the wallet back into her pocket. Longwell had been
the first one on the scene after Kathy's girlfriend had
discovered her body.

Was that a coincidence?

It was becoming less and less likely.

But still, she couldn't bring herself to believe the
man would have anything to do with the girl's murder.
They had a history together. She knew him, he was a
cop, for God's sake. A good one, albeit somewhat
laid-back. He'd been over to the house more than once
for one of her father's parties.

A strong feeling of betrayal cut through her with
sharp, pointy teeth even as a small voice in her head
warned her not to get ahead of herself.

Her gut had a different feeling.

"Can I go back now?" Klein was asking.

His tone broke through. "Sure, I'm sorry to have
bothered you." She took a card out of her breast
pocket and held it out to him. "Listen, here's my card
in case you think of something else."

Klein looked at her pointedly. After a beat he accepted the card, shoving it into his own pocket. "You don't want to know what I'm thinking now."

"Thank you for your help," she murmured mechanically as Klein walked away.

The moment they were out of earshot, on their way outside, Cole asked, "The cop he pointed out, how well do you know him?" he asked again.

She still chewed on the information, trying to make sense out of it. Longwell hadn't said anything about knowing the woman. *Had* he known her, or was Klein confused because he'd seen Longwell on the premises after Kathy's body had been found?

She let the cold air hit her, bracing her, hoping it would somehow help her sort everything out and put it in its right place before she answered. "I went to the academy with him."

He opened the door on her side. "Could he have done it?"

Rayne sat down, waiting for him to join her. "I would have said no, but then, I would have said my mother was dead, too."

Getting in behind the wheel, Cole put the key in the ignition. Her last comment had come out of nowhere and threw him. "Your mother? What does she have to do with this?"

The words had just slipped out, she hadn't meant for them to. Now that they had, she struggled with the right thing to do. To bury them until she had time to figure out just what to do about her discovery—if it actually *was* a discovery.

But Rayne could feel this ache inside of her, this

very great need to share these thoughts, these feelings with someone, before she exploded. And he was the only one around.

She looked at him, saying something she'd never thought she'd hear herself saying, not after all the heartache that had come before, not after she'd resigned herself to what she'd thought was the inevitable.

''That woman in the diner. I think she might be my mother.''

Chapter 13

Cole eased his foot off the brake and put the car into drive. "What do you mean, you think she's your mother? I thought you told me that your mother was dead."

She'd made peace with this belief after years of struggling with her emotions. But now doubts assailed her. She almost wished she had never walked into that diner.

"They found my mother's car in the river." She recited the events in a staccato, detached voice. It was the only way to keep her emotions from overwhelming her. "She'd gone over the side. The weather had been bad. The conclusion was that she'd lost control of the vehicle." The words hurt despite all her precautions. "The M.E. ruled it an accidental death by drowning."

She sighed deeply. "But they never found the body and my father never gave up hope that she was alive."

By now, he'd picked up enough about the Cavanaughs to know how close they were. He didn't see a mother walking away from all that, not willingly. "If she was alive, why wouldn't she come home?"

"I don't know."

She'd snapped the retort and then flashed Cole an apologetic look. Her nerves were definitely on edge right now. Between possibly ruining her career with this investigation, putting herself emotionally on the line with Cole and now seeing what might be a ghost from the past, she didn't know just how much more she could take.

"They'd had an argument, but it wasn't anything that would keep her from coming back. My mother always went for a drive after an argument, claimed it cleared her brain." At a loss, Rayne shook her head. She kept trying to connect the dots and her pen kept running out of ink.

"And you think that woman's your mother."

"Yes. No," she corrected quickly, then looked at him helplessly. She just wasn't sure. But there was this gut feeling nagging at her "She's the right age and there's something about the way she looked when she smiled—" Rayne stopped, knowing how absurd, how "out there" she had to seem to him. "I know this must sound crazy to you. Maybe it is crazy, but—" She turned to look at him. At least he wasn't laughing at her. "I just can't shake this gut feeling."

It had been with her all the way to the bed-and-breakfast, haunting her.

"Send your father out."

That would be the simplest solution, but she hesitated even thinking about it. "I don't know. I don't want to put him through all this, get his hopes up if I'm wrong. She said she'd never heard of the Cavanaughs when I asked her. If she was my mother, could she look at me and say she didn't know who I was?"

They were approaching a long, winding road. Because of what had happened so recently, Cole tested his brakes, first gingerly, then with force. They held. He continued down the road.

"You were the youngest, you changed a lot in the last fifteen years." He glanced at her. "Hell, you've changed a lot in the last ten."

All to the good, he added silently.

Rayne grappled with the feelings that were scattered all throughout her.

She felt vulnerable. And the way he'd just looked at her made her feel more so.

Desperately in need of someone's arms around her.

What the hell was happening to her? she upbraided herself. Was she coming completely unraveled? Here she was, flying in the face of convention, thumbing her nose at her fellow officers and maybe her entire career, and now she thought her mother had come back from the dead after she'd finally managed to bury the woman in her heart. On top of that, she was treading in places she'd never expected herself to be. There were feelings, real feelings, beginning to surface inside of her, feelings that had nothing to do with family or duty, or loyalty.

And they were scaring the hell out of her.

She rotated her neck, trying to feel less stiff, less tense. It didn't work. "Maybe I'm just on edge."

"Maybe we both are," he agreed.

God knew ever since he'd come back into town, he felt as if someone had peeled away the sheathing on his nerves, exposing every one of them to the elements. To fate. He found himself feeling things for the first time in a long time, something other than detached satisfaction, the way he did whenever he saw the outcome of one of his projections: a family with a home of their own, usually for the first time in their lives.

Charity and a desire to do right by those less fortunate was involved there. None of that had anything to do with what he was feeling right now.

As if he didn't have enough going on, he mocked himself.

"Maybe you should go back after this is over," he was careful to specify because Eric's fate was on the line, "and ask around about this woman."

"I already did. At the diner. The cashier said she and 'Claire' were tight, that they'd been friends ever since she came into town fourteen, fifteen years ago."

"What was her history before then?"

She shook her head. "The woman said 'Claire' never talked about it."

He could see Rayne's reasoning. That did tip the scales toward what she was thinking. "And you're sure there would have been no reason for your mother to want to disappear?''

''I'd stake my life on it.''

Cole slowed the car as they approached a sharp curve. The road back seemed to be all inclines. ''Amnesia,'' he said suddenly.

''What?''

It seemed the only plausible conclusion. ''Amnesia,'' he repeated. ''Maybe that woman in the diner *is* your mother. Maybe she's had amnesia all this time and that's why she never came home.''

That was a plot device used in particularly poor movies made for television, she thought, frowning. ''That's kind of thin, don't you think?''

''Not so thin. There's medical data to back that up.'' Out of the corner of his eye he saw her looking at him quizzically. ''I do a lot of reading on planes. Not too many magazines to choose from,'' he explained. ''Don't forget, your mother was in a traumatic accident. When her car went over the side like that, she probably thought she was going to die.'' He knew how harrowing it could be, coming face-to-face with your own mortality. ''Scrambling out of a would-be watery grave could send anyone out of their right mind.'' He spared her another look as the road temporarily straightened itself out. ''Amnesia comes not just from a blow to the head, but from experiencing some kind of severe emotional trauma. I'd say going over the side in a car bound for the bottom of the river qualifies.''

It made sense, she supposed. It would explain why her mother—if she was her mother—had looked right at her and not seen anything, felt anything that she could discern by the woman's expression.

She had just one question. "Why are you trying to talk me into this?"

"Not trying to talk you into it," he contradicted. "I'm just trying to talk you out of turning your back on something until you have all the facts."

It was the most elementary of reasons, and she should have realized it herself. Rayne frowned, looking out the window. "I'm a cop, I should know that."

He wondered if she was always this hard on herself. "You're a person and not quite as perfect as you'd like to believe."

Rayne looked at him sharply. She sat up in her seat. "I don't believe I'm perfect."

She caught the smile lurking at the corners of his mouth. "'Quite' as perfect," he corrected.

He was trying to help her out with her problem when she should have been trying to help him with his. The clock was ticking for him. For her, it had long since gone into overtime.

Exasperated with herself, she tendered what she hoped passed for an apology. "God, here I am, spilling out my guts to you and completely ignoring why we came here in the first place."

He hadn't forgotten and he really doubted that she had, either. But this was something that was troubling her, that she needed to work out. Hearing her share it with him had placed him in a very odd position. An intimate one he both welcomed and felt uneasy about.

This wasn't casual anymore, this thing that was

buzzing between them that neither of them wanted to name. Hell, if he were being honest with himself, it never really had been casual. Though she tried to give off that impression, Rayne Cavanaugh was by no means a casual woman. She was the kind of woman who hollowed out a place for herself in your life and stayed there, even long after she'd physically left.

He could already feel pieces of himself being chipped away.

"We're on the road back," he noted. "Nothing we can do about it until we reach Aurora again."

He'd be lying if he pretended that the information they'd just obtained from Kathy Fallon's upstairs neighbor didn't excite him. It renewed his hope that they could find whoever it was that had killed Kathy.

Someone other than his brother.

Mentally, she'd already reached home. "When we do, I want to go to the Shannon." The Shannon was the local hang-out located near the precinct. The one where all the police personnel went to let off a little steam at the end of the day in an attempt to dull their senses and forget what they had seen on the dark side of the streets. "Longwell hangs out there."

He nodded. "Sounds like a plan to me."

Longwell wasn't there.

They arrived after five. Rayne knew that the police officer's shift ended then and he always capped off his day by stopping here, at least for one beer. It was a habit he rarely broke.

The moment she walked into the noisy bar with

Cole, Rayne noticed that the very atmosphere seemed to change. The din lowered considerably.

It took very little imagination to believe that every single pair of eyes had turned in their direction.

Trying not to be obvious, she looked around the crowded room for a sibling, or a cousin, or at the very least, a friendly face. The best she got was impassive.

There was no family to be found here tonight, real or artificial.

Shoulders braced, she walked up to the bar. The bartender, Raul, a devote weight-lifter and the brother of a man in blue, raised a brow in her direction.

''Beer?'' he asked.

Before she could answer, Cole reached over her, putting down a ten on the bar. He held up two fingers to underscore his request.

''Two,'' he said.

''Tap?'' Raul looked from Rayne to Cole. Both nodded their assent.

With a shrug, the bartender poured two mugs from the beer on tap and set them on the bar. Foamy heads slid their contents down the side as he took the ten and made change.

Rayne leaned over the bar, not wanting to raise her voice if she could avoid it. ''Have you seen Longwell?''

''Nope.'' Leaving the change on the bar, Raul moved to the other end. One of the customers was waving to him.

''Not very friendly,'' Cole commented.

He was, usually. Which only meant one thing.

A voice coming from the other end confirmed it. "Word gets around."

Turning almost in unison, they looked to see a uniformed officer standing several feet away from them. Rayne recognized the man as Longwell's partner, Roy Williams.

Cole knew menacing when he was confronted with it. "What kind of word?"

The other man took long, cold measure of him as his brown eyes swept over his torso. Cole already knew what the verdict was. "That someone's looking to stir up trouble."

Rayne held up her hand, placing it on Cole's chest and stopping him as he stepped forward. He was about to defend her, she could see it, could almost see the heated words rising to his lips.

But this was her fight and she was nothing if she couldn't be her own person. She looked at Williams coldly. She'd never liked the man. The feeling was mutual. "I'm not looking to stir up anything but the truth."

Williams sneered. "You've already got the truth. Now I'm sorry you can't deal with it," the officer told Cole, "but your little brother killed her and we've got him dead to rights."

She moved again, placing her body between the two men. She could tell Williams wanted to take a swing at Cole and the latter was not going to just stand still and take it. "You're Longwell's partner."

"Yeah." Williams spat out the word contemptuously as his very look dared her to make something of it.

"You with him when he called in Kathy Fallon's murder?" She hadn't seen his name on the report, but if he was there, then she had questions for him.

But Williams shook his head. "Doctor's appointment." And then he picked up the banner for his partner. Loyalty demanded it. "I didn't have to be there. Everything went by the book." He leaned in, his manner just short of menacing. "Those of us who don't have relatives to get us promotions are real careful not to mess up things like that."

Rayne could feel her blood beginning to boil. She'd been through this before, heard the accusations that because her father was the former chief of police and her uncle was the current chief of detectives, she'd had an easy time of it.

That was strictly jealousy talking, but knowing didn't help curb the anger she felt. She could feel it flaring now.

"Look, just because the only better place your relatives could help you get is a higher rock at the zoo, don't take it out on me," Rayne countered. Wanting desperately to flatten him or at the very least, to wipe the smirk off his face, she struggled to regain control. "I just need to talk to Longwell."

"He's out of town today. His father's sick, so he took some personal time. You know about personal time, don't you?" Williams sneered, his eyes shifting toward Cole before returning to her face. "Some of us don't use it to help twist the evidence."

Cole'd had about all he could take. He knew that saying anything at all was just playing into Williams's hands, but he couldn't just stand here, listening to the man mouth off at Rayne without saying something, *doing* something.

So he got into the man's face. "Why don't you just quit while you're ahead?" He saw the contempt in the other man's face. "While you still have all your teeth in your mouth?"

It was exactly what Williams wanted. He puffed his barrel chest out and looked around the room in triumph. "You must be really stupid, Garrison, threatening an officer of the law in front of witnesses."

"I'm not threatening, I'm making an observation," Cole said easily, though his voice was steely. "Nothing wrong with that."

"Okay, that's enough. Break it up."

To her surprise, it was Patterson, her own partner, who came up to step in between the two men and separate them. She knew for a fact that while Patterson liked Longwell, he had very little respect for Williams.

"No reason to throw your lip around, Williams," he said. "Cavanaugh just wants to talk to her former partner, that's all." Patterson looked at Cole pointedly. "Right, Cavanaugh?"

Cole did his best to look innocent, even though they all knew he was more than willing to take a shot at separating Williams from his attitude. "Right."

"Well, he's not here," Patterson told him, then looked at Rayne. "Won't be back until tomorrow, maybe the day after. Now why don't you take any other questions out of here?'' he suggested, talking directly to Rayne.

The words were strict but the look in his eyes, for the first time that she could recall, was kindly.

To ensure her compliance, Patterson purposely walked out the door with the two of them.

But once they were outside, it was another story. His quiet demeanor flew out the proverbial window.

''What the hell is wrong with you?'' Patterson demanded, his ire reserved for Rayne. It reminded her of a hundred similar scenes she'd played out with her father when she was younger. For the first time, she felt as if she and Patterson had finally made a connection.

''You have a death wish?'' he railed. ''Right now, until this thing goes to trial, Cavanaugh or no Cavanaugh, you're a pariah in their eyes. You should know better than to go waltzing in there—even with a bodyguard.'' He jerked his thumb in Cole's direction.

She heard only one thing and it wasn't blotted out by his loud words. Thanks to her father, she'd become fluent in grumpy. ''Thanks for sticking up for me.''

''I'm not sticking up for you, I'm sticking up for me,'' Patterson corrected her. ''I'm your partner. Guilt by association, remember?'' He looked at Cole. ''And you, you're lucky they didn't tear you apart. You're the enemy. Anyone who threatens the reputation of the boys in blue is the enemy,'' he underscored.

And then he paused as twenty-seven years of being on the force came to the fore. ''What do you want with Longwell, anyway?''

It was best not to let anyone know she and Cole suspected Longwell of doing more than his duty in this case. "Just need to get some things cleared up," she answered.

Patterson shook his head. The look in his eyes told her he knew better. "You're as closemouthed as your old man." He snorted. "Must be hell at your house when it's just the two of you." He looked at his watch. It was getting late. "I got a wife and a burnt dinner waiting for me. Thirty years and she hasn't learned how to cook," he grumbled, walking away.

Cole lost no time in getting them back to his car. They were living on borrowed time in more ways than one. If Williams followed them out, there was no telling where things could end. He'd do his brother no good from the wrong side of a set of bars.

"I want to talk to Kathy's neighbors again," Rayne told him the moment he got into the vehicle. "Show Longwell's picture around."

It didn't take a genius to know what was on her mind. "You're going to ask them if they noticed Longwell coming by a lot?"

She nodded. "There has to be one busybody in the complex to confirm what Klein told us."

That was going to take more time and who was to say the one person they might want to talk to would be in just then? "Got a better idea," he told her as they pulled out of the parking lot. "Why don't we check her phone records against his?"

She blew out a breath. "I should have thought of that."

"You would have," Cole assured her. "Eventually."

It was dark in the car, but she could have sworn she saw him grinning. Or maybe she just felt him grinning, felt the way his mouth moved as it curved.

She turned on the radio in self-defense.

They went to his hotel room. Rayne immediately got busy with Cole's computer.

The sophisticated programs she found loaded on the hard drive took her breath away. They weren't anything that could be found in the average businessman's bag of tricks.

She nodded her thanks at the cup of coffee he put down beside her. "Just what business did you say you were in, again?"

"Remodeling," he told her glibly. "But you never know when you might need some extra information."

In her wilder days, she'd gone with a computer genius who liked challenging himself by hacking into hack-proof sites. His hobby had eventually landed him behind bars, but not before he'd taught her a few things about the art of making a computer perform mind-boggling feats.

She paused, her fingers poised over the keyboard. She thought like a cop these days, even at times against her will. "This is illegal, you know."

He needed answers now. And no one needed to know they'd done a dry run first. "The law has gray areas. You can get a proper warrant in the morning and do this again. Right now, we need to see if we're on the right track. No sense in bothering a judge for no reason.''

In his place, she knew she'd use the same reasoning. ''Okay, let's see if there was any phone talk that led to pillow talk.''

As she set about getting into the phone company's records, Rayne tried to recall if there'd been anything in Longwell's manner that should have alerted her. But there hadn't been any indication that he was hiding anything, only that he resented her questioning his findings. At the time, she'd chalked it up to his pride, not any kind of apprehension on his part.

Was she wrong then?

Or was she wrong now?

There was more than one phone company to choose from and some had better safeguards than others. It took her a while, but she finally found what she was looking for. With triumph, she pointed to the screen.

''Kathy Fallon and Longwell definitely talked on the phone. There's a total of twenty one-minute calls between the two once she took out her restraining order on Eric and I haven't even looked into their cell phone calls.''

His hand on her shoulder, Cole leaned to look at the screen. He'd been less than three feet away the entire time she'd been conducting her search. At times, it was a little hard concentrating on what she was doing. The man was working his way under her skin.

''She could have been calling him about Eric.''

She looked at him in surprise. She would have

thought he'd jump at this information, not try to discount it. "Whose side are you on?"

"Just playing devil's advocate."

She typed in another combination of keys, preparing the program she'd hacked into to bring up Kathy Fallon's cell phone account. "I'd say you had that down pat, at least the devil part."

And she was playing with fire, without an extinguisher in sight.

She felt something for Cole Garrison, had always felt something, however recessed she'd tried to keep it. And if she wasn't careful, it was going to upset the order she'd always kept her affairs in.

Cole turned her chair around so that she faced him. Something quickened inside her stomach, but she brazened it out. "What are you doing?"

They'd been at this all day and for the most part, they'd been successful. But there was little more they could do, officially, until at least the morning. That left them with the night. And he knew what he wanted to do with it. "The devil has this very strong urge to play."

She could feel her pulse revving up. "Is it overwhelming?"

He smiled into her eyes. What *was* it about this woman that made him want to throw all caution to the wind? "Several notches above overwhelming."

She rose to her feet, her body coming in instant contact with his, sliding along it as she straightened. Electric waves undulated all through her. Telegraphing messages to the desires that were threatening to ravage her if she didn't do something about them.

"Can't have you causing havoc if you don't get your way."

Taking the hem of her sweater, he pulled it up over her head and then discarded it to the side. He'd been envisioning the way her breasts rose and fell, unencumbered by clothing, all day. "Nope."

Not to be outdone, she yanked off his shirt, sending it to the floor. "I'll guess I'll just have to make the sacrifice to save mankind."

He grinned and created a tidal wave in her stomach. "Very noble of you."

She inclined her head, humor curving her mouth. "I'm a noble kind of girl."

She felt his fingers brushing against her abdomen as he undid the button of her jeans. "Noble is not what I'm looking for right now."

She grinned, her invitation clear. "Then why don't you scratch the surface and see what happens?"

Chapter 14

The look in his eyes undulated its way into her system. "Scratching isn't exactly what I had in mind, either."

"Oh?"

Rayne shivered with anticipation as he opened the clasp behind her back. Her bra slipped forward. Sliding his thumbs along the swell, Cole coaxed the lacy blue material away from her breasts. She could feel everything quickening inside of her.

Ready.

"And just what did you have in mind?" Her mouth felt dryer than the desert after a three-year drought. The words all seemed to stick together on her tongue.

"Why don't I show you instead?" He tugged down her slacks.

She stepped out of them, hardly daring to breathe.

The next second, her pulse was racing as he grasped her buttocks, kneading the firm flesh to him. She could feel the hot imprint of his body against hers.

"I'm not very good with words," he told her.

If her heart raced any faster, she could swear it was going to pop out of her chest. To keep from gasping, she measured out each word separately. "I guess you tend to be better with your hands."

There was a hint of mischief in his eyes. "You tell me."

As he kissed her, his fingers began to explore the inner core of her, each movement bringing her closer to the edge of a climax.

How did he manage to do that so fast? Was it her anticipation that urged the process on so quickly? It seemed as if she was halfway there from the very first moment he touched her.

His chuckle vibrated against her lips, echoing in her head. She didn't stop to ask if he was laughing at her, her needs were too great. The only thing she was aware of was that she wanted him. Wanted him now, before she erupted.

Like a huge, overwhelming celebration, the first climax exploded within her even as she struggled to get Cole's jeans off him. It was disorienting and wonderful. Temporarily forgetting everything else, she shuddered, her body moving against him as she gloried in the sensation he'd created for her.

And in moving, she was causing earthquakes to begin inside of him. Kicking his jeans aside, Cole lost no time in pursuing the vein of pleasure. Swiftly he pushed her back on the bed, then began to weave a network of exploratory kisses over her entire body, leaving imprints of his lips, his tongue, his teeth everywhere.

Rayne twisted and turned, moaning his name, moaning things that remained, for the most part, unintelligible to both of them.

When she arched against him in open invitation, Cole accepted it in his own fashion. Rather than forge the union she silently begged for, he held himself in check a little while longer. For the sake of their mutual gratification. So instead, he continued anointing her body.

The circle of openmouthed kisses grew dangerously close to her core. When his tongue finally darted in, Rayne was certain she couldn't handle the exquisite sensations that were assaulting her body.

She wanted them to stop.

She wanted them to continue.

But most of all, she wanted him.

Forever.

Cole had the upper hand here. No matter how much she wanted to deny it, to make it equal, or take control, it was Cole who held that position, Cole who reduced her to a pulsating mass who could barely think. The only consolation she had was the moan that escaped his lips when she grasped him, her long fingers stroking him. It told her that the ecstasy that was being created was not strictly one-sided.

And then, just as swiftly, he entered her and they

were joined together. Together, the way she felt they always had been.

The way she wished they always would be.

She found herself cleaving to him in ways she had never imagined before. Heart and soul. Body and mind. Completely.

She'd never been happier in her life. And never more afraid.

When the final explosion came that took them both over the top, Rayne held on to him so hard, she thought her fingers would snap off.

He waited until his heart had settled down to a peaceful beat instead of a vibrating drumroll before he trusted himself to roll off her. Before he ventured saying anything.

With a huge satisfied sigh, he cradled her against him and thought of absolutely nothing, just leaving himself tucked into the moment. When she stirred, he pressed a kiss to her forehead and surprised himself. He hadn't thought that he was capable of tenderness, and yet he'd taken to it like a duck to water. It felt good.

"I've been wanting to do this ever since the last time."

Fears began to grow inside of her. Tiny fears that threatened to obliterate everything. She felt herself scrambling inside to hold them at bay. A farm girl armed with a pitchfork against nuclear warheads.

"Don't say last time," she begged quietly, "Don't say next time. There's only now. This time."

"Living in the moment?"

She could feel herself growing defensive and knew that she shouldn't be. "It's all any of us know we have."

"I used to feel the same way. Until I started helping people find their future." Looking down at her, trying to see her expression, he said, "There's nothing wrong in planning for tomorrow."

That was where he was wrong. She let out a shaky breath. "There is if it doesn't come."

This was about her mother and he knew it was something she had to work out for herself. He could only be there for her when and if she did. Pulling Rayne to him, he began making love to her once more, slowly this time, so that they could each savor the moment.

Her body began to heat again, even though she would have sworn in any court of law that every fire, at least for now, had been summarily extinguished. "What are you doing?"

"Tipping the scales in my favor," was all he told her before he kissed her.

When he woke up, night enshrouded most of the room. He turned into her only to find the place beside him was empty.

Had she left?

Bolting upright, he realized that a soft humming came from the area of the desk. A soft humming and dim lighting from the single lamp she'd switched on to the smallest setting.

Rayne sat in front of his laptop, deeply engrossed

in whatever she'd managed to pull up on the screen. She wore his shirt, the ends seductively brushed up along her thighs. He was willing to bet she didn't have anything on underneath.

He could feel himself wanting her all over again.

Taking care not to make any noise, he slipped out of bed and walked up behind her. She appeared to be so taken with what she was reading, she didn't seem to hear him. He smiled to himself and gently slid his hands along the sides of her neck, caressing her throat.

"Come back to bed," he urged softly.

Startled, she jumped beneath his hands.

"Hey, easy," he soothed, then laughed. "I thought cops were supposed to have nerves of steel."

"Right now, mine are mush."

And turning softer by the minute, she thought as she turned to look at Cole. He was as naked as the day he was born and a hell of a lot more magnificent. But she couldn't afford to be sidetracked, not now. What she'd discovered had to be shared.

"I think I found something."

Raising the hair away from her neck, Cole pressed a soft kiss there. "So do I." And it might just be the rest of his life, he thought. The concept was beginning to become less and less frightening the more he thought about it.

If she didn't get him to stop, she wasn't going to be able to think in another moment. She could already feel herself responding to him on all levels.

With superhuman effort, she moved her head away. "No, I'm serious. It's about Eric."

That caught his attention. Straightening, he looked at the screen. "What?"

She had a nagging little feeling that she'd over-looked something basic. Maybe it even was the reason why she felt she had to look into the case against Eric. She'd finally been able to pull in the vague memory that had been playing hide-and-seek with her mind. It was just a brief moment, really. Eric sitting beside her in English class, writing notes.

"Eric's left-handed, isn't he?"

He wasn't sure what that had to do with anything, but he nodded. "For the most part, yes, although he does do some things with his right hand." When she raised a quizzical brow, he explained, "He broke his left arm when he was ten. With his arm in a cast, he had to learn to use his right hand. Never got very good at it. Why?"

She wanted to follow this line of thinking for a second. "So to the casual observer, Eric might seem right-handed, just like a good deal of the world."

"Right..." Dragging the word out, Cole waited for her to make her point.

"I just looked at the autopsy report again." She didn't bother telling him how it had found its way from the M.E.'s computer to his. The less he knew about that, the safer he was. "And—" She couldn't continue. "Damn it, Cole, please put on some pants. I'm having trouble stringing words together."

"I'm sorry." But the grin on his face as he pulled on his jeans told her he was no such thing. Zipping up, he waved for her to continue. "Go on."

"Among other things, the autopsy report describes the fatal stab wound—left to right, the way a right-handed person would do it," she enunciated carefully. "A left-handed person would deliver the blow from right to left. We still may not know who did do it, but it's for sure that Eric didn't kill her. The initial thrust wouldn't have been as deep as it was."

Overjoyed, Cole bracketed her shoulders with his hands and scooped her up from the table. He kissed her mouth long and hard. Leaving them both more than a little breathless.

"That's for Eric," he told her.

She grinned, very satisfied with herself. "Kisses pretty good for a man behind bars." Rayne glanced at her watch. It was a little past two. She doubted if anyone from the D.A.'s office could be roused at this hour. She knew that Janelle could, but she didn't want her cousin going out on a limb for her. The limb belonged to her alone. She'd carved her initials into it. "Now I'd like Eric's brother to kiss me, please."

Cole slipped his arms around her, pulling her closer to him. "No sooner said than done."

He found he didn't need his jeans for long.

They split up.

By seven Cole had already gotten in contact with Eric's lawyer, rousing him out of bed. Holland stopped complaining bitterly when Cole explained what they had uncovered about the fatal wound that had killed Kathy Fallon. In short order, he made arrangements to meet with the lawyer at the D.A.'s office within the hour.

Watching him hang up, Rayne made her decision. There was something she needed to do. "I'll hook up with you at the police station."

Her announcement caught him by surprise. He'd have thought she'd want to be there every step of the way. "Aren't you coming with me?"

She shook her head. "Not right away. I have to go home." She'd given this a lot of thought, wrestling with her conscience all night, when she hadn't been wrestling with him. "I have to tell my father what I found out." She could guess what he was going to say. "I know it's been fifteen years and another few hours isn't going to matter, but—"

"Go," he told her. "He deserves to know, to go see this woman for himself."

She had no idea why she felt so relieved to hear him support her decision. Even now she was plagued with doubts about it. "I just hope this isn't going to turn out to be a wild-goose chase—"

"Only one way to find out." He flashed an encouraging smile at her. "I'll see you later." About to leave, Cole stopped and crossed back to her. Taking hold of Rayne by her shoulders, he kissed her soundly, then forced himself to release her. They both had errands of mercy to run. "Good luck."

She nodded. "To both of us," she added after he'd shut the door.

Andrew didn't bother to look up when he heard the back door open.

"You missed breakfast again." He'd just finished

putting away the last of the dirty dishes into the dish-washer. Flipping the dial, he began the wash cycle. ''This is getting to be a habit.''

She stared at his back. How was he going to react? Would this be too much for him? And what if it *wasn't* her mother? Now that she was here, she could feel some of her bravado, some of her convictions, slipping away. ''Twice isn't a habit.''

''Okay, it's the beginning of a habit,'' he allowed. Reaching for a towel, he wiped his hands. ''You going to split hairs with me?''

She was stalling, she thought, because she was afraid to say the words out loud, afraid of it not being true. Afraid of hurting her father the way he'd been hurt so many times before.

When she didn't answer, Andrew finally turned around to look at her. The moment he did, he read the expression on her face. Everything inside of him came to attention. ''What's wrong?''

''What makes you think anything is wrong?'' Her voice no longer carried with it the conviction that had infused it only a few years ago. Over time, she'd lost some of her false bravado.

Andrew found he was short on patience this morning. He'd spend the night worrying about her and the morning thinking he was too old for this kind of thing.

''Cut the stalling tactics, Rayne. Whether you like it or not, I can read you like a book. A mystery novel sometimes, but—''

There was only one way to get this said and that was to blurt it out. "I think I saw her."

"Her?" He looked at Rayne, the word echoing in his chest. Mocking him. His thoughts converged in one direction, but he couldn't believe that his daughter meant what he wanted her to mean. There was caution in his voice as he said, "Who?"

Rayne took a deep breath, trying to steady nerves that had come out of nowhere to take control. The word still came out shaky.

"Mom."

Her father looked at her for a moment that stretched out so far, so thin, she could almost hear it creaking. There was no other sound in the room. No music, no cars passing outside, no birds singing. Nothing.

"Say something," she begged.

Exercising extreme control, Andrew held himself in check. He didn't trust his voice beyond a single word. "Where?"

Now that she'd begun, the words came out in a flood. "Up the coast, on the way to Bainbridge-by-the-sea. She's working at a diner." Her words played back in her head. "I know this sounds crazy—"

He pulled her over to the table, motioning for her to sit down. He dropped into the chair opposite her. His knees felt as if they were hollow.

"Crazy. That's the word everyone used because I refused to believe she'd drowned." He took her hand in his, as if that could form some kind of bond that would transfer any detail she might forget to include. "Tell me everything."

"There isn't all that much to tell."

She went through it quickly, telling him how she'd spoken to the cashier and that as far as the woman knew, "Claire" never mentioned anything about her childhood, or anything that had happened in her life before she'd come into the small town.

Her father listened to her intently, as if each word was a secret to be investigated on its own before it was gathered together with the rest.

Finishing, she looked up into his eyes. "I wasn't sure if I should tell you—"

Because they were so alike, he knew exactly what she was thinking, exactly the path her reasoning had taken. Vacillating between distrust and a desire for it to be true.

"You had to," he assured her.

Now that she'd told him, she wanted to protect him from any disappointment that loomed in front of him. "I don't even really know for sure that it's her, Dad." She paused, debating. Then told him what had persuaded her. "But there's this feeling—"

He understood perfectly. "Never underestimate gut feelings, Rayne. It's kept many of us alive." Getting up, he crossed over to the counter and took a sheet of paper from the pad he always kept there. "Tell me exactly where this diner is."

She gave him the directions. He wrote them down, then folded the paper and put it in his pocket. "You're going there now?"

"There's no reason to wait."

None but fear, he added silently.

Part of him wanted to hold on to the information, to revel, just for a little while, in the possibility that he would finally, after all these years, find Rose. If he went there now, once he walked into that diner all that might be taken away from him.

But he'd never been a man to hang back when moving forward could accomplish something.

She followed him to the front door. "Want me to come with you?"

The car was going to be full as it was. Filled with his nerves. It was better if she didn't see him this way. He smiled at her, but shook his head. "Thanks, but I'd rather do this alone."

She understood. "Dad—"

Hand on the doorknob, he paused to look at his youngest. Rayne threw her arms around his neck and held him for a moment, praying that things would turn out the right way. Praying that her father would be lifted out of limbo. She didn't even begin to think about the way finding their mother alive would affect the rest of them. It was too soon for that.

"Good luck," she murmured, brushing her lips against his cheek.

Andrew nodded, not trusting his voice. His throat was suddenly clogged with emotion. Touching her cheek with his fingers, he silently told her how much he loved her.

And then he was gone.

Rayne stood in the foyer for a long moment, praying she hadn't just sent her father off to have his heart broken again.

Dragging a deep breath into her lungs, she turned on her heel and raced up the stairs. She was giving herself exactly fifteen minutes to shower and change into fresh clothing.

Rayne was out the door in just under fourteen.

Checking the pockets of her jacket for keys, she hurried to her car. And stopped dead the second she saw him.

Longwell was getting out of his car.

The vehicle was parked right in front of her driveway. From the sounds it was making, he must have just pulled up. Which meant her father hadn't seen him before he left. An uneasy premonition reared its head. Rayne slipped her hands into her pockets.

"I thought you were out of town." The words were a challenge. Her eyes never left Longwell's face. He looked far from happy.

There was no one else out. Everyone had left for wherever they were going, school, work, shopping. Rayne felt suddenly alone and exposed. She cursed the fact that she didn't keep her weapon in her pocket. All she had within easy reach was her cell phone.

Longwell's fair face reddened a little more with each step he took toward her. "What the hell do you think you're doing? It's not enough to question my findings, to make it look as if I did something wrong, now you're trying to pin this on me?"

He'd taken one hell of a leap from point A to point B. Innocent men didn't think that way. "I'm not trying to pin anything on you—"

"Don't lie to me, Rayne," he growled. He was in

her face now, fairly snarling. "How much is that pretty boy paying you to plant evidence?"

She had no idea what he was talking about and doubted that he did, either. Cornered animals lashed out indiscriminately. Had they cornered him? "I'm not planting evidence, Longwell. Why don't you just calm down and maybe we can—"

"No! 'We' can't do anything. Me, I'm going to do something, not you, bitch. You women are all alike. I thought you were different, honest, but you're just like the rest, conniving, looking out for yourself, sucking a man dry and then throwing him away—"

He was rambling. She tried again, putting her hand on his arm. "Longwell, look, whatever's wrong—"

Without warning, he grabbed her hand and yanked it up high behind her. She bit down on her lip not to cry out from the pain that went shooting up her arm right on up to the top of her head. For one second, she thought he'd broken it.

Grunting orders, Longwell pushed her toward his car. There was no way she could twist around and get out of the hold he had on her. The more she tried, the harder he tugged her arm behind her until she felt dizzy from the pain.

"No more talking," he growled at her.

"Longwell," she cried, raising her voice. "Longwell, you're not making any sense."

Fisting his hand, he hit her square in the jaw. "I said no more talking."

Rayne barely made out the words as she crumpled and slipped into darkness.

Chapter 15

Her head and face were throbbing badly and it felt as if her eyelids were being held down with ten-pound weights as she struggled to open them. A moan nearly erupted from her lips but she managed to stifle it at the last moment. She needed to get her bearings. All she knew was that she was moving.

A car, that was it, he'd taken her to his car just before he'd surprised her with that sucker punch.

She finally managed to pry her eyes open.

She was right, they were in a car. Longwell was driving. She could make out the hilt of a gun tucked into his waistband.

For a second she thought of lunging for it, but her wrists were bound in front of her and she was held down by the seat belt Longwell had strapped around her, more to hold her prisoner than for her safety.

Can you hear me, Cole? Are you listening? Please be there, she prayed. She cleared her throat. Her head ached harder. "What are you going to do with me?"

Longwell didn't answer the question directly. Glaring in her direction, he had the crazed look of a man who'd been pushed over the edge. He pushed down harder on the accelerator.

"You brought this on yourself, you know. Just like she did. Why didn't you just keep out of it? It wasn't even your case, damn it," he railed. "Rollins and Webber wrote off on it, why couldn't you?"

Good, he was shouting. She raised her own voice. "Why did you kill her?"

She saw Longwell grip the wheel harder, his knuckles almost white. "I didn't want to. She made me. She wouldn't shut up." Incensed, it was as if he wasn't even in the car with her anymore, but back in Kathy's apartment, confronting the woman. "First she made me fall in love with her, then she dumped me. When I asked her to give us another chance, just another chance, she laughed at me. Said I was worse than the last loser." He shook his head, as if the events were all a mystery to him. "The only reason she dumped Garrison was because his parents had cut him off." His voice went flat. And sounded all the more menacing. "She shouldn't have laughed at me."

More, she needed more. "What about the ring? Did she give you Eric's ring?"

"Yeah, she gave it to me. And then she wanted it back. So I gave it to her." He laughed. "Just not the way she wanted it."

"How did it get back to Eric's apartment? Did you put it there?"

"Yeah, I put it there, when we made the arrest." He looked at her. "You're never going to be able to tell anyone this, you know."

He was going to kill her. Rayne's mind began to race, at war with the pain that was assaulting it from all directions. "We can take your story to the D.A., Longwell. It was a crime of passion, there were extenuating circumstances, they can take that into consideration."

His eyes told her he knew how that worked. "And what, give me twenty instead of life? Don't you understand?" he demanded, his voice cracking. "I can't do any time. I'm a cop, for God's sake. You know what they do to cops behind bars."

She could almost feel sorry for him. The man was desperate. Maybe as desperate as he'd been when he'd gone to plead with Kathy Fallon to take him back. She tried to appeal to his sense of logic. "If you kill me, there aren't any extenuating circumstances to hide behind. It'll be cold-blooded murder."

"I can't do time," he insisted again. His voice bordered on hysteria that was barely being kept in check.

She kept trying to loosen her bonds, pulling her wrists apart as hard as she could. They weren't budging. "So where are you taking me? The river?"

The laugh sent a cold chill down her spine. "Hey, it was good enough for your old lady. They never found her body."

She had to clamp down on the flood of emotion that

threatened to overwhelm her. To die the same way her mother reportedly had, the irony almost undid her.

Think, Rayne, think.

"Why didn't you dump Kathy's body there?"

There was pure disgust in his voice. "I wasn't thinking."

"And you're not thinking now," she insisted. "Stop while there's still time, Longwell."

"There *is* no time," he snapped back. "It's too late to undo what I've done." His manner was frenzied now, like a man who found himself boxed in and was frantically looking for an opening to squeeze through. "But if I get rid of you and that pretty boy who stirred everything up, then maybe I've got a chance."

She tried again, fighting to stay calm. "Your only chance is turning yourself in."

"That's a bunch of crap and you know it!" he shouted at her.

She looked around. They were on their way out of Aurora. Was this the route her mother had taken that day? Rayne felt sick down to the pit of her stomach. She had to keep stalling, had to somehow get Longwell to listen to reason. It couldn't end this way. She had too much to live for.

"Damn it, Longwell, this is me, Rayne Cavanaugh. We went through the academy together. Don't you remember, we were even partnered together when we first got out. You can't just kill me."

For a moment he looked as if he genuinely regretted what he had to do, but he had his back against the wall. "Look, I'm sorry, really sorry. If there was any

other way, I'd take it. But there's not.'' He looked in
his rearview mirror just before he started to take the
turn that would lead him onto the road that would
eventually lead him to the river. Longwell stiffened.
It was obvious that something he saw upset him. ''God
damn it.'' He bit off a string of curses. ''Where the
hell did he come from?''

Even as he asked the question, he stomped down
on the gas. Trapped in her seat, Rayne tried to crane
her neck to see who was behind them. Unable to turn,
she looked in the side mirror instead. A flood of relief
washed over her.

Thank God. Cole had picked up her signal, the one
coming from her cell phone.

''Give it up, Longwell,'' she urged softly.

He looked at her with eyes that appeared to be half
crazed. ''Okay, we'll both go over.''

The speedometer was climbing, hitting seventy,
then eighty and going beyond. Dread replaced relief.
She knew that if Longwell got to the bridge, he was
going to go over the side, killing them both.

Just like your mother.

Suddenly, like bees gathering in the distance, the
sound of sirens began to fill the air. At first faintly,
then stronger and stronger as they came closer. Rayne
saw the panic on the policeman's face and immediately realized that he was going to still try to find a
way to kill them both.

Her hands were bound together as tightly as ever,
but she managed to lunge for the steering wheel. Grab-
bing it, Rayne pulled as hard as she could, turning the

car sharply to the right. They fought for control of the wheel. The car fishtailed from side to side like a drunken sailor on weekend shore leave after six months at sea.

Cars coming from the opposite direction swerved frantically to get out of the way. Tires screamed, melding with the curses that spewed out of Longwell's mouth. Suddenly the car flew over a curb, turned sideways and crashed into an SUV parked on the side before it finally came to a shuddering halt.

Rayne remembered hitting her head, or maybe it was her mouth. She tasted blood.

And then the driver's door was being yanked opened and Cole filled the space.

"Rayne, Rayne, are you all right?"

She felt as if she'd been thrown head-first into a blender, but she was alive and that was all that mattered. And he'd heard her. He'd come. "Never better." She managed to somehow get the words out.

Cole dragged the semiconscious rogue cop out of the car. He wanted to kill Longwell, to strangle him with his bare hands. But even now, the police cars with the people he'd called were converging all around them. To vent his rage, Cole settled for delivering one good, swift punch to the man's jaw.

Instead of swinging back, Longwell crumpled at his feet.

The passenger door was wedged against the SUV. There was no way he could get to her that way. Cole crawled in on the driver's side and, as quickly as he could, got Rayne untangled from the seat belt. Afraid that the shattered windshield might collapse on her at any moment, he lost no time in getting her out.

She winced as he pulled her across the bench seat. "Are you sure you're all right? He didn't hurt you?" he demanded. Faint blue markings were starting to set in. "Your face is beginning to bruise."

Right now, it felt like a throbbing mass and her eye seemed about to swell shut. "He knocked me out to get me into the car, but I'm okay."

The instant Cole had her out of the wreck, a squadron of questions fired at her from all directions. Her mouth dropped open. Every member of her family who was actively on the force had shown up, siblings as well as cousins. The only one who seemed to be missing was her uncle Brian.

She looked at Cole. "What did you do?" she asked.

"When I figured out what was going on, I called Shaw and told him Longwell had kidnapped you. We tracked your cell phone signal." Not wanting to cause her any more pain, he squashed the urge to hug her to him. She'd kept her head in a dire situation. Cole felt relief and pride mingle within him. She was one hell of a woman. "Pretty smart of you to call me and leave the line open."

She smiled and then instantly winced because it hurt her lip. The moment she had seen Longwell coming toward her, the hairs had stood up in the back of her neck. The way they always did when she had a premonition. She'd slipped her hand into her pocket and pressed the automatic dial button for Cole's cell phone, praying that Cole wouldn't start talking before Longwell did.

"Saw it in an old Harrison Ford movie. I figured if it was good enough for Harrison Ford, it was good enough for me."

Her cousin Troy was the first to reach her. "Rayne, are you all right?"

"What the hell did he do to you?" Clay demanded hotly.

"You're lucky she's still alive, Longwell." Shaw jerked the man to his feet, only to have the policeman crumble to his knees again. Shaw had been in the first vehicle behind Cole. He looked at him now. "Hey, just how hard did you hit him?" There was no mistaking the admiration in his voice. "Not that the bastard didn't deserve it."

Now that it was over, the pain was sinking in in earnest. Rayne sagged a little against Cole. "Longwell's got a glass jaw," she told her brother.

Her cousin Dax cocked his head, looking at her face. "Speaking of jaws, Rayne, maybe you should go have that lip looked at."

"Yeah," Clay put in, then grinned broadly at his younger sister. "Maybe the doctor'll tell you that you can't talk until it heals."

"That kind of stuff only happens in fairy tales," Teri lamented.

Callie placed a protective arm around her. There was unmistakable relief in her smile as she looked at the youngest in the group. "Knowing Rayne, she'd find a way to become a ventriloquist."

They were using humor to defuse a very tense situation, Cole thought. It was evident that they were all very aware the youngest among them had been a hairbreadth away from becoming a casualty today.

But she hadn't and that was what they were all focused on now.

"No doctor," Rayne said firmly. She would have shaken her head if it didn't hurt so much.

"Too late," her other cousin Jarred told her. He jerked a thumb behind him at the ambulance that was even now making its way toward them.

Rayne groaned. She hated hospitals, hated the thought of being poked and prodded at. "Send it back," she insisted.

Cole surprised her by taking hold of her arm and saying, "You're going."

His tone left no room for argument, at least, not for the average person. But anyone in the family could have told him that Rayne was anything but average. It was close to impossible to get her to do something she didn't want to do.

She dug in. Her hero swiftly became her nemesis. "The hell I am."

Cole didn't waste time arguing. Actions, as far as he was concerned, always spoke louder than words. As the ambulance came to a halt and the others watched, he scooped Rayne up in his arms.

"Yes, the hell you are." A paramedic hurried out of the cab, making his way to the back of the ambulance to open the doors. As he walked toward the vehicle, Cole glanced over his shoulder toward the group behind him. "Can someone see to my car?"

"You got it, sport," Dax called out. He grinned as he looked at the other members of his family. "Looks like Rayne might just have met her match."

"Works for me," Shaw commented as he yanked Longwell back to his feet again. This time, the man managed to stand up long enough to be handcuffed and deposited into a squad car.

Refusing to lie down on the gurney, Rayne sat on it instead. The paramedic had finished administering to her over her obvious glare. She would have waved him away if Cole hadn't stopped her.

She didn't like not being able to call her own shots. And yet, having someone looking out for her did carry with it a strange sweetness she was almost afraid to explore.

"This is a waste of time," Rayne insisted. "It's just a cut lip."

In response, Cole took her chin in his hand, tilting her head so that he could get a better look at it. Her bottom lip had swollen around the cut. Hints of yellow were beginning to join the ghost of blue along her cheek. "And a hell of a bruise forming."

"I can put ice on that and my lip." Talking without moving her lower lip too much was proving to be a challenge, but nothing she wasn't up to. She shifted impatiently on the gurney. There were reports she should be filling out.

"There's no need to go to the hospital."

Cole crossed his arms and looked at her. "Do you have to argue about everything?"

She sniffed, watching the streets go by. Feeling powerless. "Only when I'm right."

Amusement twisted his mouth. "And how often are you wrong?"

She glanced in his direction. "I'll let you know when it comes up."

Damn, she was making it sound as if she could just turn toward him anytime the whim hit her, Rayne thought. Nothing could be further from the truth. Cole wouldn't be there to turn to, at least not soon. His reason for coming back to Aurora was gone now. She knew that because of what Longwell had confessed in the car on the open line, the D.A. would be dropping the murder charges against Eric. With his brother free, Cole could go back to his life again.

And away from her.

The thought stung far more than either her lip or her cheek. But there was nothing she could do about that. He had his world and she had hers. Besides, he'd never asked her to enter his world and she couldn't very well just ask him to stay in hers. That would be presuming too much.

Suddenly she didn't want things to end. "You should give me your e-mail."

He looked at her, confused. "Why would you want that?"

"So we can stay in touch with each other once you leave town." Even that had a desperate ring to it, she thought, upbraiding herself. Damn it, where was her pride? "You know, drop each other the occasional note around the holidays, things like that."

He took a good long look at her. So long that she was about to ask him what was wrong when he had a question of his own for her. "Are you trying to give me the bum's rush?"

Talk about getting his signals crossed, she thought. "What?"

"You have me leaving town," he pointed out. "Who said anything about leaving town?" He certainly hadn't mentioned it.

Did that mean—nope, hold it, don't go there unless you're sure the ground isn't going to open up beneath your feet. So instead, she lifted her chin defensively. "Well, aren't you? The only reason you came back to Aurora was to help Eric clear the murder rap and now Eric's going to be released. Case closed," she announced with unmistakable finality.

They took a corner and the gurney moved a little. He put his hand out to steady Rayne.

"You're right, that is the only reason I came back to town. But I've been thinking, maybe I can find a reason to stay." His eyes washed over her, caressing her. "What I do is pretty mobile, but I can have a central base of operations anywhere."

Her heart suddenly accelerating, Rayne made the natural assumption. It almost felt like it came out of a fantasy. "Here?"

"Maybe." He struggled to keep a straight face. "If I find a good enough reason to stay."

Rayne could feel her breath hitching itself in her

lungs. "And what do you consider to be a good enough reason to stay?"

He pretended to think. As if this hadn't been forming in his head from the very beginning, even without his knowledge. "Well, if I had a house here. Or better still, a wife here, that might do it."

Stunned, she stared at him. She'd thought he was just talking about staying in town, not anything more. "A what?"

"A wife," he repeated. "You know, kind of like a husband, except shorter and prettier." He resisted the temptation to trace the outline of her mouth with his tongue, the temptation to take her into his arms and kiss her soundly. "Know where I can find one?"

She reminded herself to breathe. Maybe she was just light-headed and that was why she was hearing what she thought she was. "Just any old one?"

"No, I've got a few requirements." He began to elaborately tick them off his fingers one by one. "She has to be fiery, has to be intelligent, and be her own person, except that once in a while, she has to realize that I'm my own person, too."

So far, it sounded perfect. But then, Cole was pretty much perfect in his own right. From where she stood, it was a package deal.

"Go on."

"I'd like her to come up to here." He hit his shoulder with the side of his hand. His eyes shifted to her face and a smile curved his mouth. "And have gray-blue eyes and curly blond hair. Oh, and legs that don't know when to quit."

God but she loved him, she thought. The black sheep and the rebel, who would have ever thought? "Anything else?"

This time he did gather her to him. "She's got to rock my world."

Did she? Did she do that for him? "I wouldn't know about that part—"

"I would." His eyes grew very serious as he looked at her. "I can't begin to tell you what went through my head when I realized that Longwell had taken you prisoner. All I could think of was that if I couldn't reach you in time, I was going to kill him."

"In front of my whole family?" she asked incredulously.

That had never been a deterrent. "Didn't matter. If Longwell had killed you, I wouldn't have anything to live for."

"Why?"

"Because I love you, that's why, damn it."

"I love you, too, damn it." She grinned broadly at him. "Now go back to the other part."

He wasn't sure he understood what she was asking him to do. "What other part?"

Her grin went straight to his heart and then to his gut. "The part where I'm filling out the application to be your wife."

He took her hand in his. He had no ring, no proper words, but that didn't stop him. "Will you?"

She wanted to drag the moment out just a tad more. "Will I what?" she asked innocently.

She deserved the full sentence. "Lorrayne Rose Cavanaugh, will you marry me?"

He knew her middle name. The thought that he'd gone to the trouble to find out filled her with a gentle sweetness. Rayne felt the ambulance come to a stop.

"In a heartbeat," she declared. "Now kiss me quick before they do something to my lower lip and I can't use it."

Pulling her up to her feet, Cole gathered her into his arms and lowered his head.

But before contact was successfully made, the back doors opened.

"We're here," the paramedic told them.

"Not yet," Cole told him. He pulled the door out of the paramedic's hand. "But almost."

As the paramedic looked on in surprise, Cole shoved the door closed again. Just before he kissed his future bride-to-be.

Epilogue

At two o'clock, the parking lot on the side of the diner looked fairly empty.

Andrew pulled up in a space that was neither too close nor too far. With slow, deliberate steps, he got out of his vehicle, crossed to the diner and walked up the two steps directly in front of the door.

He paused for a minute, his hand on the door handle, bracing himself for disappointment. So many times before it had assailed him, sneaking around corners, robbing him of his prize. Every time he thought he had a lead, a clue, a path that would finally unite him with Rose, he found himself looking at a dead end.

And yet, he never gave up, never turned his back on the small kernel of hope that refused to vanish. Refused to give him peace.

"You going in, or you just gonna stand there like a statue, blocking everyone's way?" a deep voice behind him demanded impatiently. "C'mon, pal, in or out, just do it now."

In. He was definitely in.

"Sorry," Andrew murmured to the man, not even glancing in his direction. The man didn't count. What was inside might.

The woman at his left immediately took his attention. Sitting behind a cash register, she was full-figured, with short, strawberry-colored hair and a ready smile that she sent in his direction.

She wasn't his Rose.

He looked around, orienting himself. There was nothing outstanding about this diner, nothing to set it apart from the hundreds of other diners that were scattered throughout the country. The counter was long and scarred, the booths old and in need of refurbishing, the menu uneventful, a duplicate of so many others.

And then everything else faded.

He saw her.

His mind wasn't on the counter or the booths or the menu. His eyes and attention were riveted to the blonde in the pink uniform at the far end of the counter. Leaning over a newspaper, she seemed engrossed in what she was reading.

His heart raced as he moved closer, then sat down at the counter.

After a moment, as if sensing his presence, she raised her head and looked up.

"Rose?" he whispered.

She flashed a smile at him, a smile that had always brought him to his knees.

"No, Claire, see?" With her thumb and forefinger the waitress framed her name tag for him. "Claire," she repeated.

There was no recognition in her eyes as she looked at him.

* * * * *

*If you liked DANGEROUS GAMES,
you'll love Marie Ferrarella's next
CAVANAUGH Justice romance,
THE STRONG SILENT TYPE,
coming to you from
Silhouette's Special Edition
in May 2004.
Don't miss it!*

eHARLEQUIN.com

The eHarlequin.com online community is *the* place to share opinions, thoughts and feelings!

- Joining the community is easy, fun and **FREE!**
- Connect with **other romance fans** on our message boards.
- Meet your **favorite authors** without leaving home!
- **Share opinions** on books, movies, celebrities…and *more!*

Here's what our members say:

"I love the friendly and helpful atmosphere filled with support and humor."
—Texanna (eHarlequin.com member)

"Is this the place for me, or what? There is nothing I love more than 'talking' books, especially with fellow readers who are reading the same ones I am."
—Jo Ann (eHarlequin.com member)

Join today by visiting
www.eHarlequin.com!

If you enjoyed what you just read,
then we've got an offer you can't resist!

Take 2 bestselling
love stories FREE!

Plus get a FREE surprise gift!

COMING NEXT MONTH

SIMCNM0204